SILENT TEARDROPS

A Novel by

Jennifer N. Shannon

Tom,

It's a pleasure working with you! You are such an awesome person! Thank you for those weekly thoughts & inspirational messages, they mean a lot! :)

Best wishes & much success,

Jennifer N.

Library of Congress Cataloging-in-Publication Data
Shannon, Jennifer N.
Silent Teardrops/ Jennifer N. Shannon

ISBN 0-9765617-0-0
1. African-American Fiction I. Title.
2001012345

This is a work of fiction. Names, characters, places, and incidents either
are the product of the author's imagination or are used fictitiously, and any
resemblance to actual persons, living or dead, events or locales is entirely
coincidental.

Printed in the United States of America

Acknowledgements...

No shout-outs I said...but life is teaching me so much and through every lesson, I'm still learning about myself and growing from it...besides, this is my first book and I'd like to thank a bunch of people but unfortunately...space and time won't allow it. Anyway, here goes...please blame the mind and not the heart!

To my mother, thank you for being my inspiration. Phrases nor words could say I love you enough!

To my family. To those who had enough faith in me to give of your criticism, financial contributions and unwavering support and encouragement! You are my foundation and I love you!

To my friends who believe in me and love me in spite of. To those who I can cry with, laugh with, be open with, and never ashamed...I love each of you and pray our friendship endures...

To the man who taught me the sincerity in loving someone. The love was always real although not always shown. Please be happy.

To the Heavenly Father. For your countless blessings, for family and friends who love me, for the mind to move forward and achieve and most importantly for knowing that through everything, good and bad, You are still in charge! Thank you!

BE SAFE, BEZ AND MAY GOD BLESS!

SILENT TEARDROPS

Part 1

James

DAMN I OUGHT to fix that screen door. It's just hanging there, waiting on one of us to slam it too hard or pull it the wrong way or whatever so it'll fall off. I don't know why I let the door sit there and be raggedy. I coulda been fixed it long time ago but I'm too lazy. Shit, I'm probably the one who broke it in the first place but I know one thing, if it break for I get to fixing it then Sheila gone have another reason to be mad at me besides the one she already got. I been gone for the past few days. Maybe it's been a week now. I don't know. I don't even have a reason why. I just couldn't stay in the house no more. She ain't done nothing to me but I go through this shit at least once a month. Yeah at least once a month I go off somewhere and just get drunk. Mostly at my buddy Charlie's juke joint called *Lucky's*. He'll usually give me some Creek liquor he got hid underneath the counter. That's one man that ain't never got problems having liquor somewhere. From Sunday to Saturday he's stacked wit booze for whatever the occasion. And you best believe I'm one of the main men sitting at the bar for some of what he got. But for some reason Charlie ain't been at the juke joint for the past three days. Nothing can keep him from *Lucky's* on a normal basis so I don't know what's going on wit him this week.

Funny thang is even though Charlie ain't been round, I still been drinking. The other bartender, Randy been hooking me up. I been drinking something a little lighter than normal though. Something that wasn't gone make me throw it back up, so I been settling for Gin. I didn't want no dark liquor cause I didn't need nothing that was gone make me feel worst than I had too. For some reason that dark shit always have me depressed and acting off the wall but usually that's all I drink. I only had two shots of the white stuff tonight. I kinda wish I had stayed and at least had a few more so I could sort of be numb when I get in the house. Numb like when you getting a cavity filled and they stick you wit that long ass needle that hurt at first but after the initial pinch wear off you can't feel nothing else. I need to feel like that. I need to be numb when Sheila start that cussing and screaming cause she bout fed up with the bullshit I keep putting her through. I know I'm wrong. I know I shouldn't be making her go through this shit but I feel so helpless. Almost like God done gave me hands but I can't use em' or like if I wanted to touch something that was right in front of my face, I can't reach it. That's how I been feeling over these last two years. Can't help it. I guess if I could've stopped everything from happening I'd feel better bout myself. It feels bad when a man can't do what a man posed too, which is protect his family. If I coulda just saved Sheila from going through what she been going through then maybe I wouldn't feel so worthless. She done got so sad now. I just look in her face and her eyes look dreary like she carrying the world right there on her back. She seems like a piece of her body gone. Like maybe she walking round without one of the limbs that she normally used to having. I feel sorry for her but I guess I feel more sorry for myself since I ain't doing no better. Hopefully she won't kick me out for good tonight but if she do I deserve it.

I start walking up the steps but flop back down on the second to last one. Not yet I think as I stick my hand in my shirt pocket. I pull out a crumbled plastic bag and put it on the step beside me. After I reach back in my shirt pocket, I get the TOP cigarette paper, tear a piece out, and lay it in my lap. I pick up the bag and open it. With my index finger and thumb I pinch a little bit of the grassy like stuff and sit it on the paper. I kinda rub it wit my finger as to spread it across and after I spread it out I pick up the white thin paper wit the marijuana on it and lick one side. I start twisting it around while I wrap the paper on top of itself. Once I'm done I hold it up in the air. Yeah, I done rolled a nice sized joint. Now where's my lighter. It's not in my shirt pocket so I start banging my hand against my thigh. There it goes. I pull it out and start flicking the switch. Come on now baby, light for daddy. After I shake it a little and hold my hand around the lighter, something on the inside must ignite cause a flame comes bursting out the tiny hole on top of the lighter. I quickly put the joint in my mouth while at the same time letting the fire hit it. I take one long pull so it'll catch hold. This is nice. Real nice. The sweet tinglely taste and smell invades my mouth and nose. As I take the joint out, I hold what smoke I do have, in my mouth and slowly let it out through my nose. This is what I do for about the next 30 minutes. Just sit here and smoke this reffa. I keep lighting it cause it's kinda windy out and if it gets blown out I just light it again and keep right on smoking. I smoke until it gets down to a real small piece. It's funny how I was never really interested in smoking till I went over to Vietnam. We were young, scared, and nervous. Didn't know enough about life and was damn sure scared of losing our own. So once the cigarettes started to become routine and reality came back, reffa was the next thang on our list. Whenever we could, we smoked. I'm pretty sure smoking marijuana was the only thing I brought back home wit me. I left my sanity, nerves, heart, soul and everything else right there in Vietnam in that war.

Damn I should roll me up another one for I go in this house. I should but I don't. I drop the roach in my shirt pocket and put all of the other stuff in my pocket as well. I use the black railing as an aid to help me up. After I brush myself off and stand up completely, I turn around and face the house. I slowly walk up the rest of the steps and gently pull the door up and then out so it won't make too much noise. I place the key in the lock, wiggle it, turn it, then I hear something click and that's when I know I can go in. Before I even walk in the house good the light comes on.

"Damn, Sheila."

"James where you been?"

"Can I at least get in the house first for you start interrogating me?"

"No. Where you been? I been worried sick bout you."

"I'm sorry Sheila, for real. It won't happen no more."

"And you said that how many other times before," she asks as she walks to the bedroom.

"I know, I done said it plenty times before but this time I'm serious. You know I love you."

Before I know it she turns around and slaps the shit out of me. After she does it, she looks bout as surprised as I am. She ain't never hit me before so she really must be mad cause she done hauled off and hit me in my face. I can't even look at her cause either I'm scared she gone hit me again or that I'm a flip out and hit her back.

"I'm sorry, I didn't mean to hit you but stop making me feel like shit all the time. I'm so tired. I'm just tired James."

"I know."

"No you don't cause you still putting me through this shit. If you knew or cared that my body and mind feel like they both gone shut down any day now you wouldn't keep doing this to me."

I can't say nothing cause I know she right. I know she having a hard time dealing wit everything but I guess I'm too selfish. I guess I'm too much in my own pain that I won't even help her wit hers. I want to reach out and touch her but she seems so distant right now. Like more on her mind than just this.

"Listen James, I love you but I don't know how much more of this I can take."

"I understand."

I turn my head and get ready to walk back down the hall. Before my body is completely turned Sheila touches my face. And not just any touch but a soft gentle caress. In the same place she hit me. I turn to face her. She keeps touching me, soft and sensual like. It's been a long time since she did that. A long time since I didn't have to beg to get some affection from her. Here she go again rubbing my face. Her fingertips are so soft and her touch is so gentle. She keeps touching me slower and gentler than the time before while looking me deep in my eyes. Sheila has a way that just turns me on. She pretty. Her face is dark and smooth, like melted chocolate. The thing that really turns me on is them eyes. Her eyes are big and brown. Her eyelashes are long and full and just accent the rest of her face. When she looks at me wit them eyes and them full ass lips, I just be bout to pass out right there. And then she tall, thick and got a big ass.

Got thighs that's just right too. Not too big not too small. Right in the middle. Her tits are kinda little but not too small for me. I mean she in a C cup but I'm a tittie man so when I see the D's and on up that's what get me excited. But overall she got just what I want and need.

"What you doing Sheila?"

"Just hush."

I do what she says cause right after she says it she kisses me. She actually slides her tongue in my mouth and moves it around. At first I just stand here feeling myself get all excited. Then I join her. I kiss her back and she likes it. Somehow we standing here but moving backward at the same time. We finally get to where we at the dresser and can't go no more. With one swipe of the hand every perfume bottle and lotion bottle and anything else that was up there is now on the floor. I lift Sheila up on the dresser and feel underneath her satin nightgown. That nightgown is the one I bought her for our wedding. Back then I loved the feel of it but now it's been washed so much and worn so much that it's old looking. It don't even feel like no good satin no more. It feels more like fine cotton. I try to ignore the thoughts of the old nightgown, which isn't hard to do cause Sheila's caressing my neck. Now she know how much I can't resist no wet feeling on my neck so now I just go on and tear them panties off. I can't even hardly wait now. I mean I do take time to unzip my pants without catching myself in the zipper. It's kinda hard to get these tight underwear down but I manage okay and finally here I am. I just kinda ease on inside her after I pull her body close to edge of the dresser. Damn, Sheila don't usually feel like this. I can't really describe it but she sure feels good. I'm moving now and I got my hand pressed on the wall so I can hold myself up. And we got this rhythm where we're both in the same motion. Sorta like we're a part of one another. I can't

stand it no more cause Lord knows I feel like I'm bought to bust wide open. Just before I

do let myself go I open my eyes long enough to see that Sheila's crying. Her face is wet

maybe like she's been crying the whole time. I want to wipe her eyes and ask her why

she crying cause at first I thought she was enjoying me the way she seemed to rock her

body wit mine but I can't. My mind and body ain't strong enough. So I close my eyes

again and release myself without much regard to whether or not Sheila's still shedding

tears. Once I'm done I open my eyes again. My legs are weak and I feel like I'm gonna

fall but I stand there and try to be strong. Sheila musta already wiped her eyes cause they

red but there ain't no more tears. I guess she didn't want me to catch her crying so she

done cleared the evidence of her wet cheeks and now she kisses me again. Maybe this

time to reassure me that ain't nothing wrong so me being the type of man I am or maybe

just a man in the first place, ignore what I just seen and hug my baby just a little tighter. I

still feel weak and tired but I hold on to her a little longer. She hold on to me a little

tighter too.

That musta been the best sleep in the world cause I really can't move. Sheila

done cooked breakfast cause I smell the bacon and now I hear her walking down the hall.

That girl got some real heavy feet cause it sounds like she stomping. When she comes in

here, she sits down on the bed and then I feel her hand on me again. I turn my head until

sheets surround my face. Sheila changed the bed while I was gone cause now that I'm

woke and my nose deep in these sheets they smell good and fresh. Like they just been

washed. She always been a clean freak. She the type that pick up right after it's already been done. It can't be no later than 9 o'clock on a Saturday morning and she already done put the stuff back on the dresser. I heard her earlier but went right back to sleep. She probably even dusted it and I know that kitchen look like somebody cooking on a spotless, new stove. Like nobody even suppose to cook on a stove that shinny. She just like that.

I wish she would stop caressing me cause that mean she must be getting sentimental. Most of the time I like it when she does it but not today. Any day but today. But Sheila won't stop. She keeps on touching my face. I guess she thinking bout me and what we been through and how we gone get through.

I got to pee so I move again. This time Sheila must think she bought to wake me up cause she gets up and walks out the room. I hear her stop in front of the guest bedroom. How long she gone do this? Damn don't go in there. I finally get the strength to get up. I lightly tap my feet on the cold floor. I slowly stand and walk towards the bedroom door. I watch Sheila play with the idea of going in the room. She reaches her hand for the knob but then pulls it right back. As she gets up the nerve and her fingertips actually touch the knob, I walk up behind her and touch her on the shoulders.

"James you scared me. I thought you was sleep."

"Sheila don't keep doing this to yourself. Don't make yourself sick cause you want to go back down memory lane."

"James I just wanted to go in there and see if I needed to clean up the room. You know I haven't been in there in almost a year and today I think it's time."

She finally turns to face me as I watch her blink back tears. Not now Sheila, please. Before I can say anything she runs in the bathroom and shuts the door. I turn around and stand in front of the bathroom. I'm still weak. I can't even get up the courage to knock. I just let my arm fall down next to my leg while I walk into the kitchen. I get out a plate and use the spoon that's on the stove to dip out some grits. They all buttery and creamy-looking so I know they good. I grab about four pieces of bacon off the other plate and scoop up some eggs with another spoon. I usually put more butter in my grits but since they look like they got enough in there already I grab the salt and pepper and start adding them to my food. I always put salt and pepper in my food even before I taste it to see if I need any. While I was in Vietnam the food was terrible and now I won't eat unless it has plenty of salt and pepper. I guess it's just a habit now. When I take the plate of food to the table and sit down I realize I'm not in the mood to eat. Today is an anniversary. We been waiting on celebrating this a whole year now. This is the day our baby boy was born dead. That's why I feel nauseous right now and feel like I can't even hold water. And I know that's why Sheila in that bathroom crying now. It was the most unbearable thing I ever had to do or say or accept. Ain't nothing harder than laying to rest your own child. I don't even want to wish that on my worst enemy cause I felt like somebody had took my heart out and still expected me to live. Maybe that's why I can't seem to come home and stay. I definitely ain't been able to go in that room. Sheila must be stronger than I am cause I can't stand the thought of looking at all that baby stuff that we never got rid of. Maybe in a week or so, I'll do it cause if I don't Sheila gone go crazy. Hell I might go crazy too. We both done been through hell and back but now we got to move on.

I decide to finally go check on Sheila but before I can even stand up, I hear screaming. I jump up, run to the bathroom and open the door. I'm scared to death at what I see. Stop it, I want to say but I can't. My mouth's wide open but don't no words come out. I'm standing here feeling helpless watching my wife stand facing the mirror scratching her face. I don't mean just scratching. I mean her face is bleeding and she crying and shaking her head. What do I do? I run and grab her from behind. I wrap my arms around her body so I can control her arms and kinda settle her down. While she still being wild and flinging her arms everywhere we fall. Now we both on the floor and she's head bunting me in my mouth. After about a half hour of us sitting on the floor struggling wit each other, Sheila dozes off. Her mind finally done shut down cause I know mine done went in and out of reality a couple of times since I walked in this bathroom. I sit and rock her back and forth. I feel like she's my child and I'm her daddy. We stay here in this position for another 15 or 20 minutes. Finally, I lay her on the floor. Then I ease my legs from underneath her and stand on my feet. I'm in speed mode now cause I run in the room and do everything in a fast motion. I slip on clothes and shoes and then I run back to the bathroom. Once I see Sheila I tone down and go back to being in slow motion. I watch her head when I pick her up. It seems like she's gone. I mean knocked out worst than I was earlier. I look at her and notice that the blood is dried and matted on her face. Her lips are dry and brittle and her eyes I can tell even though they closed are red underneath her lids. I don't wipe her face; I just look down at that nightgown and wish I could tear it off. I hate that gown. I don't change her clothes I just go to the closet and pull out my old trench coat and drape it across her body. Next, I go back to being in fast motion and take Sheila to the car. Then I go back in the house, grab the keys off the counter, run back outside, get in the car and back out the driveway.

John

WHAT THE HELL he mean my baby done had a nervous breakdown. What he do to make that happen to her? I swear I'll kill him if he did something to hurt Sheila. I can't even imagine what the hell done happened. What could I have done to stop this? Maybe I coulda been there more or talked to her more or even played wit her more. I don't know but there shoulda been something I coulda done. Deep down I knew this would happen to her. I knew Sheila woulda been the one to have a nervous breakdown in front of the mirror, watching her mind walk away from her. I knew it woulda been her cause she was nothing like her momma. She was just like me. Even though Annabelle had the same thing happen to her, it wasn't her fault. I coulda stopped it from happening to her. But I wasn't man enough. And I've lived to regret it every since. Now I regret it even more cause my daughter going through the same thang my wife went through. And my wife was the strong one. But that night everything had gotten to be too much. She couldn't be strong no more and I don't blame her. I probably woulda broke long time ago. And no matter how much time passes, I can't get that out my mind. Coming in the door and seeing her face bleeding but the whole time she was smiling like wasn't a thing wrong. Then all of a sudden she got out of control and started swinging her arms and head. And I'm sure James did the same thing I did when I saw Annabelle. He probably grabbed Sheila from behind. It must be the natural thing to do cause that's the only thing I could think of. And everyday after that has been a constant reminder of what kind of man I was. And now what kind I still am.

I'm driving like a bat outta hell. It takes about an hour and 45 minutes to get down to Columbia and I been driving for less than an hour and I'm already in Camden. That means I'm almost there. I can't wait cause I swear if that James done made my baby go crazy I'm gonna kick his lil skinny ass. I really do like the boy but sometimes I can't stand him. He got my baby all messed up in the head. She can't function without him. No matter what he put her through she right there. Annabelle was nothing like that. She was sweet. But at the same time she was quiet and secretive. She kept everything to herself. Sheila the same way.

Here I am. The "Mental Hospital." There go James standing outside walking back and forth and smoking on a cigarette. He looks pretty bad. He look like he done seen a ghost or something. I pull in the first park I find and hurry out the car.

"James what the hell going on," I scream as I slam the truck door.

He walks toward me but waving his hands as if to signal me to calm down.

"John, she fine. She just had a nervous breakdown."

"Tell me something I don't know. Why the hell did she have one?"

"Listen to me John, I didn't do nothing to her."

"You better not. I'll kill you boy if I ever find out you done put yo hands on Sheila. I mean that."

By this time I'm standing directly in his face, looking down at him as if to say, I'm bout ready to beat your ass. He slowly backs up.

"John, I don't know what happened, she cooked breakfast and you know how everything been since we lost—"

He starts crying. He's trying to talk but I can't understand a word he's trying to say. I grab hold of him and give him a hug. He hugs me back. He even drops the cigarette out his hand. We just stand here out in the parking lot holding on to each other until I think he done. I don't cry cause I need to be strong some kinda way. So I hold in my tears and once he seem like his all dried up I pull him away from me.

"James, everything gone be alright. Sheila gone be fine."

"Thanks John. I don't know what I would do if I had to be down here by myself. I'm just so scared. I know we ain't been all that happy but I'm gonna change and do better. I promise."

"You got to do better. Sheila need you. Something else like this happen and it gone kill her. And if something happen to my—"

"Don't say that. Everything gone be fine."

"Well, where is she?"

"They done got her settled in a room but only one of us can go in at a time. I done been in but I came out to get some air."

"Well, I guess I need to go head and see how she is."

"Alright, I'm just gonna stay here til you get back."

"Okay. How you get in there?"

"Just go over to that side door and the lady'll tell you where she at."

I walk wit my head bowed towards the door he pointed me to. I really don't know what I'm gonna say to her. I ain't never been much of a good daddy. I mean I was there, I worked to make sure food was on the table and clothes was on they back but I didn't have the right things to say. I always felt that was they momma job. She did good till she died and then Ruthie, my oldest daughter, left home. I couldn't stop her. Didn't even want to. So I let her go and then watched Sheila's life run away from her, too. One minute she my little girl then the next she married and bout to have a child. All that was too much for me to hold on too. I already didn't know what to say to them so when she came to me and said "Daddy, I'm getting married," I almost passed out. But I handled it the best I knew how and said, "Congratulations." Other than that I didn't really know how to talk to my children, so now I'm going in a room with my baby girl and I don't even know how to express myself. I wish I could tell her I love her and that I believe things gone get better. That I believe she gone get to have that baby she seem to want so bad. I want to tell her that no matter how things looked or seemed in the past I always loved her and never meant to hurt her.

I can't think of nothing to say so I stand at the side entrance till somebody starts walking towards the door from the inside. I open it before the curly headed woman gets a chance to even reach for the knob and nod my head as if to say hello. I walk to the front desk and see another white lady sitting behind the desk. She's fat cause she looks awful wide and is eating some potato chips while she looks me up and down.

"Mam, I'm looking for Sheila Davis's room."

"And may I ask your name."

"Yeah, I'm her father, John Smith."

"Okay, you got 20 minutes in there wit her cause she got to take her medicine."

"Yes Mam."

The fat white lady told me Sheila's room was the first one on the right. I walk down the gray hallway and peek in the window on the door. She's lying in the bed. I slowly open the door and walk in.

"Sheila baby, it's me your daddy."

"Daddy, that you?"

"Yeah baby. How you?"

"I'm fine."

She starts crying. What I'm posed to do? I'm not used to her crying. She reaches her arms out for me and I finally run over to her and we embrace.

"Don't cry, it's alright. Everything gone be alright."

"But daddy, you ain't posed to see me in here like this. I don't even member what happened. And just look at me. I know I look bad cause my hair all over the place and my cheeks burning like they got holes in em."

I look her up and down and rub her forehead. I see the bruises but don't say nothing. We just sit here the entire time while I hold her in my arms. I even try to hum her a little tune Annabelle used to sing when she would be washing clothes or dishes or something. I guess Sheila likes it. She's calmed down and is now resting in my arms. For once I feel proud of myself. It feels good to have my baby girl laying in my arms relaxing and not worrying bout nothing. I feel like I done something right by Sheila and Annabelle. I know Annabelle looking down on me smiling.

After Sheila falls back asleep, I try to lay her back down without waking her up. I slowly get up and kiss her on the head and then walk out. When I pass the fat lady, I guess I'm posed to sign out or something cause she tells me to stop. I go back, put my signature on the visitor sign-out line and walk out. Once I get to where me and James first met up, I see him now sitting on the ground shaking back and forth.

"James, I'm out."

He jumps up.

"She doing alright?"

"She's alright. She fell asleep while I was in there."

"Yeah she did that to me today too."

"Well man they bout to give her some medicine so you might as well get ready to go on home."

"I will but I'm gonna at least tell her good night and that I'll probably be back tomorrow."

"Well, don't tear up that car running up and down the road. She'll be alright."

"I know."

"Well, I'm about to go. You gone be alright?"

"I'll be fine."

I shake his hand and look straight to my truck. I can't bear to be here no more. Once I get to my door and get in the truck, I hurry and put the key in the ignition. I turn the key and pat the gas at the same time so it'll crank. Then I leave. I can't even get out of Columbia good for I start crying. I just can't stop. After I looked at Sheila and saw her face looking just like Annabelle's did that time, I almost lost it. She looked so afraid. Like she saw something I didn't.

I drive slow. I'm not in no hurry to get home. Once I drive into the driveway maybe two hours later I feel like shit. I feel like I done failed as a dad. I know I ain't the best daddy but I only did what I knew how. I learned from my daddy. He was the one who spanked our butts and worked in the fields and took care of the household. He put food on the table and kept us in decent enough shoes and clothes for us to look like we had family somewhere. Hell, I don't blame him for being tired all the time and not taking the time to talk to us bout stuff we needed to know and for not making us smile when we looked sad. We just learned the best we knew how. I thought that was how it was supposed to be, so I hope my children don't blame me cause I didn't do everything right. I was just doing what I knew. Shit, I didn't blame him when he knocked me upside my head wit a steel toe boot and damn near made me pass out cause he was frustrated. It hurt but not bad enough for me to want to be mad at him cause I understood. I could look in his face after he done been outside riding on that tractor from sun up to sun down and see that he was miserable. Honestly I felt bad for him. Like he didn't deserve no life like that and my momma, poor thing she woulda been lost without him. I guess I took after her. I mean I'm stern like my daddy. I'm hardworking and wit enough education to sign my name and read important papers enough to understand them. Other than that I felt just like my mommy when her other half passed. Confused and scared. Almost like I couldn't make it on my own. Like a child learning to survive without his parents.

That's how I feel without Annabelle. Alone. But I met another woman that been coming over the house lately. It ain't the same, though. I think I'm just passing time. I don't love her or nothing but I enjoy the company. Her name Edna. She nice and she can cook alright. Her sweet potato pie taste real good but Annabelle could cook anything and it be good. Like she done put her foot in it. I cook most of the time myself. I watched Annabelle so much that I learned how to cook just by watching her. Sometimes while I would be standing there in the kitchen studying her every move, she'd try to tell me and teach me what to do. I learned but not like her. I'm pretty good but ain't nobody never seen me cook cept for Edna. She alright. I guess I'll stick wit her for a while.

I done been sitting in this truck for bout 15 minutes. I get out and walk up to the house. I guess Edna done been by cause the screen door ain't shut all the way. I don't understand why she always comes to the door when she don't see my car. Maybe I'll go see her tomorrow. But first I got to get up the nerve to make this phone call.

Ruthie

"Chris, baby wake up."

He doesn't move. He's acting like he's asleep so I graze my tongue up towards his ear.

"Stop Ruthie."

"No," I say in a seductive voice as I continue caressing his neck, while my hand rubs downward on his stomach.

"Ruthie I don't feel like it," he says while grabbing my hand before it gets any further.

"Why, you always feel like it. What's the problem today?"

"I just don't feel like it."

Just as I turn my body so that my back is touching Chris's the phone rings.

"Hello," I say as I reach over Chris's body to pick the phone up off the receiver.

"Ruthie that you."

"Yes. Daddy is that you?"

"Yeah."

"Well how you doing daddy?"

"I'm fine. I'm just calling cause you need to come home."

"What is it daddy?"

"Well yo sister, Sheila done went and had a nervous breakdown."

"Oh no, daddy. Tell me what happened."

"I just told you, Sheila went crazy and she in the nut house down in Columbia. This is a family emergency and since you ain't been home in all these years, I think it's time that you come on home and check on yo sister."

With that being said, what else can I say but "Okay."

"Alright then, call me and tell me when you gone get in and I'll come get you from the train station."

"Okay."

"Bye."

"Bye."

And that's the end of it. I get off the phone with my dad and lie back to back with Chris. I lay deep in my pillow and try not to think about the life I left behind. The people I walked away from without looking back. Without any warning a sharp pain runs through my stomach. My body jerks as I instinctively go to the fetal position. This is the second time this week. They're now coming more often and deeper. Something's got to give. I slip out of bed and walk to the kitchen. I get a cup and pour a little bit of ginger ale. A little soda always helps when I get these pains. Once I swallow most of the acid I go get back in bed. Chris still doesn't move so I get comfortable enough to nod off into a halfway peaceful sleep.

*****

One week later and here I am sitting on a train. The Silver-star. I'm listening to the hum of the train gliding on these metal tracks. It's seems like forever since I been home. Since 1968. I left two weeks after my momma died. Just picked up and left. Moved up to Philly and didn't look back. I just couldn't stay there anymore. When momma first got sick I knew if something happened to her, I'd leave. And after Sheila called me and told me to come home from work cause momma was sick and it wasn't looking good, I prepared myself for my change. By the time I got to the hospital she had already passed. I felt so scared and so alone. She was all I had. She kept me sane. I remember it so clearly. I walked in the hospital with a lump in my throat and a churning in my stomach. I didn't even get in the sliding doors good before Sheila met me at the door with that look in her eyes. That look that said it was too late. I didn't even ask, her tears said enough. I just stood and embraced my sister but it seemed like I was just there watching the whole scene as if it was a movie playing in front of my eyes. I stood in that spot so long it felt like. Maybe it was more like my mind was still. It didn't move for a long time. I walked around in a daze, in everyday life probably for years to come. That's why I left. Living in that house without her made me nauseas. So I left and moved in with my mom's sister until I was done with school. Nobody came to my graduation. Just my aunt. Sheila sent me a card. I knew she would have come if she could. All I cared about was getting a real job and supporting myself. And it wasn't as hard to get work up north. Up there they at least gave you a chance. Down south they was just waiting on you to fail. Waiting on you to come in their establishments and businesses and ask them for a job, so they can look at you like you crazy. Before I moved I had been working as a library assistant at the elementary school. They didn't respect me. I was smart, pretty, and black. The White women were doing everything to keep me from moving up to the teaching position once I had my degree. I didn't want to be there anyway and momma's passing gave me the perfect reason to leave. She was the only reason I stayed. I would've left right after my high school graduation if she hadn't begged me to stay. She kept saying things would get better but I think deep down she knew they wouldn't. She knew that my daddy hated the sight of me no matter what was said or done. I don't understand it. It seems like every since I was born he's been at my throat. Telling me how ugly I was or that I was fat or stupid or fat again. He's insulted me everyday I can remember. If he spoke to me it was an insult. And I tried. I swear I tried to be a good daughter. I didn't give him no trouble. I didn't talk back, didn't ask him for nothing, didn't do nothing that normal kids don't do. I think the only time he said something nice to me was on my prom night. Too bad that was years ago and he hasn't said anything remotely nice to me since then. And now it's not even that he says anything bad. It's worse now cause he doesn't say anything at all. When I call home it's *hey, bye, how ya doing*, but other than that he don't even call on my birthday, or Christmas or Thanksgiving. He treats me like I don't exist. And it hurts. It makes me sad that I don't have no kind of relationship with my dad, that's probably the reason my relationship with everybody else is messed up. It's like I don't even know how to communicate properly with people. And if I do get to where I got something special with someone, I fuck it up. The first time I thought I was in love or needed to be, I didn't know how to handle it. Fucked that one up big time.

It was back during my second year at Lincoln University. I think I had about a year and a half to go. I met all kinds of nice people and I just had a ball. It was an experience I wouldn't change for anything in the world. That's when I met Henry. He was maybe a year or two older than me and was an engineering major. Time we met, we hit it off. We used to go to the drive-in, walk to class together and eventually we did everything together. It was so refreshing. So good being with someone I knew cared about me. I knew he loved me cause he showed me. But I was young. I still hadn't seen what I needed, to know that I was supposed to be with him. Especially not forever.

I probably could've still been with him now but my mind wasn't there. So much happened between us. And I couldn't help it if I had never felt like a man loved me. Was that my fault? The other reason I couldn't be completely with Henry was because there was someone else I met around the same time who made me feel like a woman too and who turned out to be my best friend. Of course that's a big part of what broke Henry and I up. He found out. And to top it all off it didn't last with me and the other person either. Not that it wasn't good but after I got in that accident I realized we could never be together. That's when I chose to be out of love. And now that Chris is asking me to let him be that one, to let him catch me when I fall, we're having problems.

I don't know what to do. I want to settle down with someone but there's so much that can happen. So much about myself that Chris doesn't know and I'm not so sure he'll be ready to accept. If I'm honest with myself I guess I do feel strongly about him, maybe even enough for it to be love. I just don't want to be hurt. Chris and I have been dealing for about a year. For the most part it's been exciting but I'm not sure if I'm ready. Maybe this is the perfect opportunity for me to get away cause we need time to step back and see if things are going to grow into something more or if we should stop this now instead of wasting time.

I hear the conductor say, "Next stop, Hamlet, NC." I immediately jump up, throw my black Agner purse over my shoulder, and stand in the aisle beside my seat. I reach inside the overhead compartment, pull down my one blue suitcase and head towards the front of the boxcar. That's one heavy suitcase. I remember when I first got it. My momma was sending me up to Philadelphia for the summer when I turned 16 so I could work. She looked at me and said, "baby, this the only piece of luggage we got so take care of it." And I did. When she died I put everything I had in this suitcase and took it with me. I still haven't invested in new luggage; I'd rather take this instead.

As the train's breaks screech on the rails, I close my eyes and say a silent prayer, asking God to help me to endure my father and to be of some service to Sheila. By the time I complete my prayer the train has come to a complete stop and a bald white man is reaching his hand up from outside the train to help me off. I grab the conductor's hand and slowly step onto the small stool and then onto the cold concrete. I guess when the conductor can tell I'm securely on the southern soil, he lets go of my hand and reaches on the train for my suitcase. It must really be heavy, because he reaches with one hand but quickly uses two to get it off the train. The balding man sits it on the ground beside me while I inhale the cool 3am air. I turn my body towards the station and before I can focus my eyes on one particular person I notice a familiar body walking towards me. "Yeah, that's my daddy," I think out loud. Once he gets a little closer, I can really see that not much has changed since I left. He looks just as handsome as he did ten years ago. His eyes are hazel, his hair is full and curly, but his 6'2 body seems smaller than I once remembered. I stand still and wait for him to get closer.

"Hey Daddy."

"Ruthie." He pauses. "How are you?"

"I'm fine," I say. I'm kinda uncomfortable but I still reach out and hug him. His large hands pat my back softly.

"So, how you doing daddy, you sure do look good."

He grins widely, showing the gold cap on one of his front teeth.

"I'm alright. Thanks. You look like you taking care of yoself too. The big city ain't doing you wrong."

"No, actually I love it."

John picks up my suitcase and I finally notice that age has indeed fallen upon him. His hands are big and strong but wrinkles have now cascaded his fingers. They're long and shake slightly as he begins lifting the suitcase. I notice that his fingernails are still long and perfectly groomed. Momma used to do his fingernails once a month and from the looks of it he's continued the tradition.

"You need some help daddy?"

"I got it."

I decide not to say anything else, cause I know the suitcase is heavy but I don't want to start off wrong. We walk along the rocky dirt driveway over to his white Ford. He throws my suitcase in the back of the truck. We go to opposite sides, get in and sit silently in the cold truck.

"Na, you know I got to let it run for a while so it can get warm."

"That's fine, I'm alright."

I sit in the car and rub the chill off my arms. Damn it's been a long time since I been in this truck. I remember when he first got it. It was the summer of 1965 and I was 17 years old. Me and Sheila were sitting on the porch, when my mom and dad drove into the yard. My mom was gleaming. She looked like she had just won some money or something. Before my dad could even shut down the engine and remove the key from the ignition, my mom was out of the truck and headed for the house. John slowly strutted behind her.

"Go head John, tell em.'"

"They can see, we got a new truck."

"That ain't all and you know it. Go head fore I tell."

"Damn woman calm down. I'm gone tell in a minute."

John looked out at the truck and then over to the brown Monte Carlo that was also sitting in the yard.

"Well, ah....well Ruthie, yo mommy and I been thinking that maybe, since you getting older now and you like going all over the world in that car over there, that we'll just go on and give this one to you and we'll just have this truck."

My eyes lit up. I couldn't believe he was saying that to me. It would've been different if my momma had said it but he was saying it. I just looked at my mom to confirm what my dad said.

I hugged them both, then ran in the house and snatched the keys from off the counter.

"Come on Sheila let's go for a ride. I can go for a ride, can't I?"

"Yeah, baby," Annabelle said after she looked at my dad. He turned his head away as my mom looked at him but there was something in his eyes. Something that made me want to cry even though it was one of the happiest days of my life. After my mom winked her eye at me and put that little bit of doubt to rest, me and Sheila ran to the car and left everything else behind.

After thinking about that story, I'm sitting in the truck smiling. I feel so happy cause I remember that as being one of the happier times I've had. And the thing was, the car was at least five years old then and by the time I finished with it, I had to pat the gas and turn the key simultaneously just so it would crank. I just got rid of the car a few years ago. It was my pride and joy. Maybe because it was the one thing my dad had given me. Maybe it wasn't all his idea and maybe even my mom lied to me with that wink, but I loved the ideal that he had given me something. That one thing was enough cause he damn sure didn't give me any of himself. Definitely not any of him emotionally and not any of his features. I guess I get my hair from him cause his is a pretty good grade and mine is a good grade. Well much better than Sheila and my momma's hair. Theirs is nappy but mine is naturally curly and soft. He definitely didn't give me any of his other features. I kinda look like my momma. I mean I'm real light-skinned so maybe he gave me that, even though he's not quite as light as me. And my momma is real dark skinned so I don't get my complexion from her. I'm only like 5'7 while everybody else in my family is tall, at least 5'9 or 5'10. I'm big for my size, too. I weigh like 165 lbs but Sheila and my momma were perfect sizes for their height. Maybe my dad did have a little to do with that cause he's a pretty big man. But on the other hand, my nose is small and my feet and hands aren't like theirs. Sometimes I don't even think I belong to this family. Maybe if I look at my dad a little harder, I'd see that I look more like him than I do my momma. Maybe that's why we don't get along.

Our 20-minute ride back home is pretty silent. Once we enter the Cheraw town limits, I notice a few changes. A few more buildings replace what used to be empty fields and old houses, and the street going to our house is now paved. Other than that I recognize everything I left behind. There isn't anything different about Cash Road. It seems like it's the entrance to Black society in Cheraw. Most of the people that live on this road or in surrounding areas are Black and are related. It's amazing how we flock together. I'm sure that came from years of slavery and dependence on each other for communication purposes. As John continues to drive down the road, he seems a little uneasy.

"You alright daddy?"

"I'm fine. I just get short of breath sometimes."

"You think you need to go to the doctor or something."

"I said I'm fine. I don't need no doctor telling me what I already know."

I don't say anything else because by that time he's easing the truck into the yard the same way he used to after he came home from work. Slow and easy. He stops before he gets to far and then he sits there for a minute after he changes the gear from drive to park. As I reach over and grab the silver lever to open the door, my dad takes a deep breath. I step onto the ground and wait on him to get out the truck. He's much slower than he used to be and he must have arthritis in his hands cause they look a little distorted. I don't stare, I just walk around to the back of the truck and hold my purse

until he gets to where I am, reaches over the cab and gets the suitcase.

When we walk to the house, he turns the knob and we go inside. He still doesn't

lock the door until he comes in for the night. Once we're in he puts my bag in Sheila's

and my, old room. As I walked through the house I noticed a new set of furniture. The

brown set is gone and now there's a flowered set still with the plastic covering each chair.

"Well Ruthie, I'm bout to turn in."

"Yeah I'm sort of tired too."

"Alrighty then. Goodnight."

"Daddy, wait a minute."

"What is it?"

I almost can't think of anything to say so I ask about Sheila again.

"When is Sheila coming home?"

"Oh, she'll be home in bout three days. I did go see her though. Only once

when it first happened, cause she looked sad and depressed."

"Well, I'll probably go down there tomorrow."

"You still know how to get around down here?"

We both grin.

"Yeah, I think I still know my way around."

"Well, just take me to work in the morning and I can find a way back home. I

have to be there at 8:00am."

"Okay, I'll be ready."

With that, we both turn and go in the opposite direction. I'm not sleepy cause I damn near slept the whole way here. Still I open my suitcase, take out a pair of pajamas and slip out of my clothes. I put on my nightgown and pull the covers back. Once I'm deep into the bed and snuggled underneath the covers I feel my body relaxing. I doze off thinking about Chris.

By 1 o'clock I'm at the Mental Hospital on Bull Street sitting in the truck. I walk to the front of the building and sign in. The halls are gray and I hear screams coming from one end of the corridor. I walk in the direction the lady told me to go but I don't go in the room. I try to peek in the window first. I see Sheila sitting in bed writing. I move my head so she can't see me and then I slowly knock on the door. I hear a faint "come in" echo from the room. I open the door and tip toe inside. I don't know why I tip toe cause it's not like she's sleep but once I do get in the room Sheila's already put her notebook away and is sitting straight up in the bed. She looks at me and her face sort of lights up and maybe mine does too cause I immediately run over and hug her around the neck. I shed maybe one or two tears and I know she's emotional cause she holds on to me entirely to tight but I don't mind.

"Hey sis, how you doing?"

I wipe my eyes before I answer. "I'm fine, the question is how are you?"

"I'm okay, just let stuff get on my nerves that's all."

"Well you know you gone be alright don't you."

"Yeah, I'm know I'm a be fine. Just fine."

We sit in silence for a while and as I examine Sheila, she keeps drifting in and out of sleep. When she wakes up, our conversation is brief but enough is said. I notice Sheila's eyes look sad when she's awake but she seems peaceful, like a baby when she's sleep. It's always been easy to tell when something was wrong with her. Her eyes are distinct that way. They're round and big, kind of glassy, and her eyelashes are long and full. And whenever Sheila's sad, bags seem to cascade underneath the corner of her eyes. Her eyeballs are so unique that she looks lost like part of her soul is wandering around on earth instead of within her body.

I sit and watch Sheila continue to nod before I finally look at my watch and realize that it's almost time for visiting hours to be over. I stare around at the gray walls that surround my sister. "What a place for my sister to be in," I whisper as I stand up and push the hard wooden chair back under the table. I lean over, gently kiss Sheila on the forehead and leave.

Shelia

Nov. 21, 1976

When I woke up Ruthie was already gone. It was so good seeing her again. It seemed like it had been so long since last time we embraced and talked. I thought the conversation was kinda dreary though. She seemed to be in another world at times, like her mind was somewhere else. And me, I just kept falling asleep cause when there's a long pause or moment of silence I just drift off. I guess it's all that medicine they got me on. It just makes me fall asleep anytime. Anyway, my sister seemed to be down and out. Maybe it was seeing me in this place. This godforsaken place cause I can't keep it together. I really don't know what happened. I member looking at myself in the mirror and as I stood there my face just looked so strange. It looked like I was different from my normal self. So then after looking at my eyes and my face, it just looked long and funny. I mean it looked so funny that I actually started laughing. I laughed until I cried, cried until I laughed. In the end I just cried. Then I started rubbing my face. I rubbed it to get the marks off. They were small circles or something. I thought I could rub them off but when that didn't work, it became scratching. I dug my fingernails deep in my face and my cheeks. I was so out of myself. It was like I was sitting over there on the tub just watching myself do that stuff. Nobody really gone understand how it feel when you are fine one minute and then the next you're losing it. I mean I was scared to death after looking at myself. Just two seconds earlier I was Sheila and then with the blink of an eye I was somebody else.

It's like I just couldn't hold anymore of the hurt and anger inside. After I had my little boy die within my body I thought I would die. It felt like someone had sucked the life out my body and just left me to live. That was something I was trying to come to terms with that day. I was trying to get over it but when I looked in the mirror everything in me changed. Not only my outer appearance but also within. I mean I've been trying not to change for a while now but somehow everything that you try to stop from happening ends up happening anyway. And James got a big part in what's going on with me. He don't see that he part to blame for me going crazy. I wish I could make him understand that I need him with me cause honestly I ain't never really loved nobody else like I know I love him. And after everything that has happened with me losing two children, it's like we done grown apart. I still love him and always will but so much has happened. That's probably why we so distant now. James don't understand why I shut down on him. I just couldn't help it. See, it didn't affect him like it did me. He don't know what it's like to have something grow inside you for months, just to die. When I had the miscarriage it was different. I mean I loved it just the same but I had only been pregnant for one month. I don't know, it just wasn't the same as the second time. If it was a boy, he woulda been named James Jr. Of course it didn't take no time to figure out who to name the boy after but we couldn't decide on Carrie or Celeste for the girl. We were all set too. We decorated the second bedroom. We had a crib in there, James painted the walls a cream color and he put little red, blue and yellow balloons all over the walls. It was so beautiful. Little teddy bears were put all over the room and in the crib. We had little baby t-shirts and socks and everything in the dresser drawer. I used to go in that room everyday and sit in the rocking chair that James got for me. He took the money he was gonna use to get two new used tires for the caddy to get me that chair. I was in my fifth month then and when I got off work he had it nice and shined up for me. It was so beautiful. He had a note on the chair.

Hey baby, this is just a little something for

the new momma. Now you can rock our baby to sleep anytime you want to. I

love you so much.

James

I cried when I saw the note. I sat right down in the chair, rocking and rubbing my stomach. And that was my routine for the next few months. I'd go sit there everyday after work. It was so relaxing and soothing. We loved it, until that night. The night I started having pains. But not the normal pains, I mean piercing pains that shot through my stomach. I hadn't felt the baby move all day but I thought maybe he needed a break cause he was tired like I was but after I had the pain I knew something was wrong. It was like three in the morning and I jumped up. James jumped up too.

"What's wrong baby?"

"I gotta go to the hospital."

"What's wrong?"

I screamed. James got out of bed, still in his draws, picked us up and put us in the car. He ran in grabbed my overnight bag, slipped on some pants and shoes and was backing out the driveway in no time. I member the look on James face. It was a mix of happiness with worry. By the time we got to the hospital, I must have passed out or something cause next thing I know James was standing over me with his head bowed and his eyes were red. His eyelashes were wet and his eyebrows were curled inward. His lips shook just a little like he was scared bout something. I just looked at him. I just couldn't think nothing bad had happened so I couldn't think nothing.

"So where is our baby," I said.

James's eyebrows curled even more and his face began to cringe with them. I think the tear is what made me worry. The one tear that fell from his left eye.

"What's wrong?"

James could hardly speak.

"Listen baby. Well." He paused for a long time before he could finish.

"Sheila baby, it was a boy. We had a boy," he said. But I couldn't understand why he crying like that. So of course I cried too. I just cried cause he was crying, cause he was crying more like a baby than any baby that I had ever seen. So just when I was getting ready to talk he fell to his knees. That scared me. He just fell straight down, grabbed me by my waist and stuck his head into my side. It hurt a little but from what I could see, he was hurting more than my stomach could ever hurt. I gently rubbed my fingers through his hair.

Boy was it nappy. He grabbed me tighter and started mumbling in my gown.

"Tell me James, I can't understand you and you scaring me."

"Sheila I got something to tell you." He took a deep breath.

"Just spit it out."

"Okay. Our boy, he didn't make it."

"What did you say?"

"He died."

The words was so blunt and dry. At first I don't think I could breath. I just looked at the ceiling and felt the tears fall. I didn't hear nothing else that James said. I don't really remember what I thought about. Not too much. I just couldn't believe it. I couldn't understand why God was punishing me. Was it something I did? I mean I did my share but. I just couldn't understand how much faith you had to have or how much patience you had to have or how much you had to go through before everything just tears you down.

I think we both cried for hours. Me without much sound. Just a cry that was more like it was deep within me instead of being loud and for the world to hear. James cried out loud. And hard. Real hard.

After that night, life for us must've fallen to pieces. Once I was let out the hospital, we had a small service and that was it. Everything went downhill. James started drinking and smoking. I even did a little more smoking. We would get high all the time. Just smoking joints nothing serious like some of my friends. Then when we weren't getting high, which was most of the time, we were fussing. We fussed about everything. About being in the bathroom too long or who was going to cook or anything. And the final straw was me. Me not wanting to make love. I just wasn't in the mood. Never. Of course I did sometimes just so we could make it through the night without the arguing but most of the time he could tell. And of course that would lead to another argument. That's more of the time when he started cheating. It was like he wasn't getting nothing from home but complaining so he went out there and did what he had to. I'm not saying it was right but I understand. I mean when I found out about it, it was him coming in the house smelling like another woman. I remember putting a knife up to his throat and dared him to come home smelling like that again. And that worked, for a while.

I'm not too sure when he had the first affair but up until now I don't think he been doing too much cheating. It depresses me. We done fussed and fussed and me threaten him but it don't work. Nothing helps us. And we so scared to loose each other that we keep going through the same thing. Right now I'm scared. So scared that it hurts. I can hardly function right worrying bout us. But somehow I think this time we gone be alright. James done been to see me almost everyday and believe it or not, no matter what we been through he sticks in there. He's a sweet man but when everything gets messed up it really gets messed up. Somehow I believe we gone be alright, though. This has got to be the wakeup call. James told me that he would lay off the weed and the drinking and everything else. I trust him. Got to trust him.

I can't wait to get out of this place. I mean I did learn a lot of stuff. They got me doing things to help me recooperate, like writing in this book but. Something about being stuck somewhere you really don't belong. I guess I'm just homesick. I just can't wait to go home and get in the bed with James and just cuddle with him. I just can't wait to get home, in my home, and visit wit my sister who I ain't seen in years. I really want to catch up wit her and see if her and daddy can get past everything that happened in the past so we can be a family. I just can't wait to get out of here.

James

SHEILA GONE BE home tomorrow. She been gone for bout two weeks and the house feels so lonely. It seems like to me the things that annoy you bout somebody is the same things you end up missing bout that same person. Sheila used to suck on her teeth and talk my head off when she got nervous. I used to say, "Can you please cut that damn noise out." Or when she used to smack when she ate. And then sometimes when I'd walk in the room, I'd walk right back out cause she would be in there picking at her feet or something. I mean ain't nothing wrong wit none of those things but they are things that when you live wit a person you just find unattractive. But I swear I miss those same things now. I miss how she used to say stuff back to me when I told her that shit bothered me. She'd say, "So, your stank feet bother me all the time, and the way you scratch me wit yo toenails bother the hell out of me." We'd end up laughing cause it was funny that we both did stuff that we knew bothered the other person. Maybe it was the reaction we got from each other that made us do it in the first place. I loved the things I hated as much as I loved her. So without her being here makes it hard for me to sleep at night. I didn't even stay home every night. I mean I ain't scared but it just didn't feel right so I went and stayed wit Mae. Most nights I stayed home and on those nights I realized that I have to change or my baby gone be dead soon. She can't keep being stressed out and me not coming home at night ain't helping her. I even told Mae that the other night. She didn't believe me though. She said that I always say that and end up coming back anyway. She probably right but I damn sure wish I could prove her wrong.

While I was home I even cleaned out the guest bedroom. We been calling it a guest bedroom even though it's been the baby room for as long as I can remember. Even when we didn't know bout Sheila being pregnant we just kinda agreed that one day that would be the room that our baby or babies would have till we could add on to the house or could afford to get in a bigger one. I don't know what made me go in there today and clean out everything cept for the bed, rocking chair, and dresser. I even redid the walls. They don't have none of that baby stuff in there no more. Just plain wallpaper. Something to cover up the balloons. At least now we can keep the door open or at least cracked without having all the memories staring us in the face. I did keep a few of the teddy bears that we bought. I put two of them on the bed and the rest in the storage room. Some of the clothes I left too cause it just didn't make no sense to throw them or give them away. One day we might get lucky or God might bless us again so I decided to leave one drawer full of clothes and the rest I emptied in a trash bag.

Now that I'm done I couldn't be in the house no more. I had to get out and I didn't feel like being bothered wit Mae, so I'm out here sitting in my car in *Lucky's* parking lot. For some reason I need something to take the edge off. Not too much just a little something.

I get out the car and slam it shut, shake hands, and slap high fives with a few men that I know and then grab the handle of the screen door. Once I walk inside, I go through the same routine of "What's jumping," or "How's it been hanging" with a few other people before I finally reach the bar. Charlie's here.

"Hey man, what's going on?"

"Ain't nothing. Where you been lately?"

"I been in and out. I heard bout Sheila man, I'm sorry."

"Thanks. She coming home tomorrow."

"Well, what you doing in here? You know you better get home and get that house clean before she want to whip on yo ass when she come home."

We both share an awkward laugh and then it seems like we're back to normal.

"Man, stop that damn talking and pour me some of liquor you got back there."

"You sure you need some of this Creek liquor? I don't want you to get tore up before you go get Sheila tomorrow."

"Charlie, I'm fine, just pour me two and I mean don't let me drink more than two. Okay."

Sure enuff, he only pours me two. Sometimes I wonder if he just don't want me to fuck up the best thing that ever happened to me or if he care bout Sheila being fucked up worst than I already am.

"Say man, what you doing for Sheila tomorrow."

"Well, I invited a few people over to the house as kinda a surprise for her, ya know. You welcome to come."

"Man I can't, cause you know how Shirley is and she want me to stay home wit the kids while she wonder off wit her girlfriends. You know sometimes I hate them damn women. They always meddling in yo business and trying to tell Shirley how she ought to be living in her own house. Man you better be glad Sheila don't be listening to all that foolishness."

"I hear ya."

"I'm telling you, Sheila a good woman and if you keep on treating her like this, it gone kill her. Cause I can't even imagine what she going through wit losing a child and all but she don't need no extra stress from you."

"Come on Charlie man, not today. You know I know how to treat Sheila and I'm gone do better. For real. I done made a promise that I ain't gone let nothing stop me from doing what I gotta for her sake."

"Alright, I'm just telling you cause I don't want to see nothing happen to her." He pauses. "Or you."

"Man I'm cool."

"Man since I ain't talked to you in a while let me fill you in on what's been happening round my way. James, Shirley done bout lost her damn mind. Besides not cleaning the damn house or cooking no decent meals, the woman pulled a fucking knife out on me bout two weeks ago. I mean she put it up to my..."

I sit and listen to Charlie talk about how his wife done tried to kill him at least three times in the last two weeks. And how he came over to the house and I wasn't there cause he thought if he didn't talk to somebody he was gonna kill her. He talks bout his children and how grown they are even though they bout three and four years old. I just sit and say, *yeah*, and *sho nuff*, and *uh huh*, just to seem like he still has my attention but my mind is wondering elsewhere. When I was walking towards *Lucky's,* I noticed, as I always do, the deep pit that sits off on the side of the building. It's the place where all the drug addicts go to get high. I've never done anything but smoke a little weed cause I've never really been interested. Something within never allowed me to step one foot down there in the hole. I mean, the hole ain't really a hole. It's more like a drop in the land. *Lucky's* sits on level ground then the land just sort of drops really low and someone got the idea to put some wooden steps going down in the hole. You should see how many people done been down there since them steps were made. I'm one of the few men who haven't. Even Charlie done stepped down there a few times which is probably the reason Shirley bout to kill him. She know just like most people that each night he smoking up almost everything he make in that same pit. While I try to concentrate on Charlie I start thinking bout my own life. I guess this little bit of liquor done started messing wit me. I'm starting to think back to when me and Sheila was happy. We used to have a good time wit each other. Used to laugh and she used to smile when I came in the door. Food would be on the table, house clean. She wasn't out there cheating on me. What more could I ask for? I know Charlie right bout Sheila being a good woman. Ain't no doubt bout that. She carry herself good and don't be out here hanging out all times a night. Sheila don't even be wit her girlfriends all the time. She would go out but more like we used to go out together. We would hang out wit other couples and have little get-togethers at our house. It used to be right. We used to be right. I really don't know how to get it back. I done got myself caught up in so much other shit now. I used to just stay round the house and hang out every now and again but now I'm drinking and smoking more. I even been sleeping wit a few more women. I don't know how to explain it. All I member is when I had to walk in that hospital room and tell her what happened to our child, the look in her eyes said it all. It let me know that everything I knew was going to be different. After the first time we lost our baby, she didn't take it that hard. We were sad and upset but it wasn't the same. And then she got pregnant bout six months later so the shock of losing the first one wasn't that bad. But when I walked in that hospital room and told her what happened to our baby boy, I could tell things were going to be different. And sho nuff, when we finally got home and settled back to our routine, things changed. At first it was okay. I mean I still had my own issues I was dealing wit but I wanted to help Sheila first. She used to walk round the house sad all the time or wouldn't go to work. All that I could understand and I even went out and got a second job at a plant to help make ends meet. But when she didn't want to have sex with me or would force herself and right after she would run take a shower and cry while she was in there, I started feeling unwanted. I mean sex ain't that big of no deal unless you addicted to it. Or unless you just like a whole lot a different women. That never appealed to me cause I done had my share and they all basically the same. I mean one or two might blow your mind but that's only if you really attracted to em' and hell I'm attracted to Sheila more than any other woman I done seen. So she not wanting to have sex wasn't the problem, it was the fact that she couldn't tell me. She didn't even trust me enough to say I can't do it yet. I mean I was hurting too and maybe it was my fault for even trying to make love to my wife after that done happened but I needed some affection too. I just wanted her to hug me and make all of what I was feeling go away. We both just sort of handled it wrong. That's when I started cheating. The first time I did it I was drunk, but I still remember.

A brown-skinned woman named Ruby walked in *Lucky's* wit a red tight fitting dress on. It had to be bout 12 o'clock cause I had already drank at least 6 shots of creek liquor and had maybe 3 or 4 beers and my high felt like it was bout to come down. So while I was bull jiving with Charlie and Bobby, here come Ruby. She came and sat down right beside me.

"Ah Bobby why don't you fix me a Hennessy straight."

"Coming right up Ruby."

"Hey there James, how you?"

"I'm fine. What about yourself?"

"I'm okay. I'm sorry to hear bout what happened."

"Thanks, but I'm alright."

"Well, where Sheila at these days, I ain't seen her in church."

"She went to visit her sister but she doing good."

"That's good. So why you in here drinking yoself half to death?"

"I'm not. I'm just out having a few drinks. Is that alright?"

"Sure is."

We sat at the bar for the next 15 minutes going back and forth till she asked me to come home wit her. I was horny as hell anyway cause I was drunk so I didn't stop to think this ain't right. All I knew was that I was lonely and the woman I loved was miles away and besides even if she would have been home she wouldn't have wanted me anyway. Ruby was there and was willing. So as she finished her drink, I flicked my wrist and allowed one more shot of liquor to burn my throat and chest before we headed out the door.

She drove. Took me to her house. The act itself was just sex. Nothing special. I didn't even look at her. Just closed my eyes and did the deed. I don't even know or care if she was satisfied. She asked me to stay but I told her I needed to get back home. By four in the morning I was sitting in the tub with all my clothes on letting water run on me. I was guilty. But when Sheila got home it became easy. She done caught me before but that didn't matter. We weren't happy. The fact was having sex with someone else is what took my mind off what I was going through. Sheila knew something was wrong but she stopped fussing after a while and kinda gave in. We still were making love but it felt different. It felt like her mind was off somewhere else. Actually the last time we made love before she did that stuff to herself was one of the few times in a long time she acted like she wanted me. Like she was right there with me enjoying me instead of acting like I was hurting her.

Back then I started sleeping wit other women cause they wanted me and showed me that they liked being wit me. Mae is the only one I stuck wit. She ain't nobody I'd leave Sheila for but she a decent lady. She the only one that don't mind what time I come over and since I know she ain't gone try to get me in no trouble, I feel a little safer wit her. She ain't that good looking but she don't fuss, she even cook early in the morning if I'm hungry, and she don't ask too many questions. That's probably the best thang bout her, she don't talk much. I mean she talk but she ain't like some of them other women who asking me all the time when I'm a leave Sheila and be wit them. They know better. I ain't leaving Sheila for no woman. Ain't no woman out here better than her so I don't know why I can't do right by her.

I look down at my watch and realize it's time for me to go home and get some rest for tomorrow.

"Ah, Charlie, I'm going to go on and get out of here for it get to late."

"Alright man. How bout one more for the road."

Charlie pours me another shot of Creek liquor. We toast to nothing in particular, just hold up our glasses and tap them against one another. With one gulp mine is down my throat burning what feels like a hole in my chest. My face cringes as I slam the glass down on the counter. After my chest calms down, I stagger off the stool.

"See ya later Charlie."

"Alright man."

I throw my hand up and walk out the door. As I go to my car, I take out a Newport and light it. Newport's are the only thing's that could calm my nerves when I got back over to the states. I tried Marlboro's, Kools, and some other off brands but Newport's are the strongest and make me feel safe for a little while. It was like if I didn't have a cigarette in my hand or mouth at least once every hour something was wrong. I turned to liquor to calm me down cause Sheila can't stand the cigarette smoke now she wishes I'd stop drinking so much. Women.

As I pass the hole, I glance over at one of the men who crawled out from the pit.

"Ah, James, what's up man?"

"Not much. What's up wit you?"

"Nothing. I heard bout Sheila. Sorry."

"Thanks."

"Ah man, here, take this."

He hands me three small rocks. I know what they are and I decide this time that I'll take them. Shit, I know how to smoke it, even seen it done, the problem is I ain't never tried it for myself.

"What—"

"Listen don't say a thing. This one's on me."

He high-fives me and walks off. I look down and stare at the wrinkles in my hand, more than the items that are laying in it. My hand is large and tough. My fingernails are thick and hard. My skin looks rough, as if I've been in several wars, not just one. Sometimes I wonder if my hands feel rough on Sheila cause they damn sure look like they probably hurt when I touch her. I continue to look down into my hand while I walk back towards the pit. I keep the cigarette in the corner of my mouth, close my fingers tightly around the drugs and then I climb down into the hole. I see a few familiar faces, some not. I look around for someone I know. Guess who I see? Charlie. He's already down here, bout to get high again. I walk straight over to him and he looks at me like he's in shock.

"Man what you doing down here?"

"Listen, don't say a word. Just tell me you got what I need to make this work," I say as I open my hand at the same time.

"Yeah," he says as he looks down.

With that, he hands me his worn plastic soda bottle with a hole on the side. A homemade crack pipe that looks like it's been used all too often. He then places a small piece of aluminum foil, and a pin in my hand. I hold my Newport while I watch Charlie carefully give me his sacred items. Once he has given them to me, he walks off and leaves.

First, I place the aluminum foil on top of the soda bottle, stick tiny holes in it, and dump my cigarette ashes on top of the foil. Afterwards, I put one of the tiny pieces of crack on top of the ashes. Ready. I then lift the 7-UP bottle towards my mouth with the hole facing me while I flick my lighter at the same time. As the fire grazes the top of the aluminum foil, I suck smoke from the side of the bottle. The first long drag is all it takes. I immediately pull the bottle away from my lips and close my eyes. Without any warning my body starts to shake as I slide down the side of the dirt wall. I sit on the ground for a while without moving. I look up and around and all I see are faces that look confused or scared. I study their faces. How their lips curl and the way their hair looks. I see women and men down in this hole and they look disturbed. They look like something's wrong. Not just like they're addicted to this stuff, more like they have to have it. The difference I see between the ones that are addicted is that one day they'll probably let go of it, but the ones that have to have it, may stop but only to start back again. They'll probably be the ones who steal from they momma and daddy to get money or they'll be the ones who don't pay they bills just to get a hit.

As a few more minutes pass the faces start looking more like they're struggling. One woman is grabbing another man's clothes, pleading for him to give her a hit. Another man's smoking, just like I had just done and another is lying on the ground beside me. He looks old and dirty. His eyes are closed and his pant leg is torn. I stare at him and quickly throw the bottle, the crack, and everything that was once in my hands on the ground. The woman that had been pleading with the man rushes to the ground as if she knows what I've thrown. Once she feels on the ground and finds everything I just had, she jumps up and smiles, but for only that one second. For that brief moment she's happy but then she looks disappointed in herself for even stooping so low. Poor thing. It's a shame she can't let go long enough to get out of this shit hole she done got herself into. Damn. What the fuck am I doing down here? I push myself up by using the wall as my support. I feel dizzy and fall back down again. I finally find a way to gain my balance and stand up long enough to function like I'm posed to. I walk towards the steps.

"James, how was it? Where ya going? I got some more if you want some."

I look into this man's face that I know I know, but somehow he looks different.

"Charlie that you."

He starts laughing.

"Damn man you can tell this yo first time cause you don't even know it's me, yo best friend."

"I'm cool man, I just gotta go."

"Alright. Get on out of here," he says, still laughing and shaking his head.

I nod and climb out the pit. I stumble to my car while people look at me like I'm crazy. Once I get to the caddy I fumble around in my pockets for the keys. I finally find them and pull them out. For some reason it's not as easy as I think to stick the key in this small ass hole. I continue to struggle with the key and look around at the same time. I feel like everybody's looking at me. Like they all standing round watching me make a fool of myself. This damn key still won't go in the lock. Did I even lock the door? I lift up the handle and there it goes, it opens. Shit, I never lock the door. What the hell wrong wit me? I try to be cool and slip in the car without people staring me down. Once I get in I can't find my keys, again. Oh, they still in my hand but I can't go nowhere. I feel like I'm gonna fall asleep. What the fuck is going on? I feel like I'm going backwards. I hope I ain't cause I know I ain't changed gears. Shit I ain't even put the key in the ignition yet. Maybe I should just sit here for a while and then I'll go home once my head stops spinning.

Ruthie

TWO DAYS IN Cheraw is all I can handle. I'm ready to go back to Philly. Today Sheila's coming home and James is having her a surprise party so I need to get mentally prepared for this gathering. If I was home I wouldn't have to deal with this cause Chris would be there to comfort me and make me feel like nothing else in the world exist. Well at least for a little while. My face lights up as I try to concentrate on something else other than him. Unconsciously I feel my right hand graze my panties and send a chill up my spine. I quickly move my hand and turn over on my stomach. I'm not comfortable. I close my eyes and feel my body report to the position it was in and my hand touch my stomach. I stop fighting what I know is about to happen and start fantasizing about Chris. The way he looks, talks, and the gentle way he caresses my body with his fingers and lips. While my mind travels back to my bedroom, my hand ventures to avenues that I'm sure are foreign to most except for Chris. He knows exactly what my body can handle and what makes it quiver and shake. My body's getting hot just thinking about it. I continue to allow my hands to feel every part of my anatomy. I start at my breast and move down past my stomach. I feel sort of silly doing this in my momma's house but I've gone too far now. Too free to stop. Like I'm riding in the wind right above the clouds. When I feel myself reaching that place of ecstasy I open my eyes and see two images looking at me, smiling. I blink my eyes, look again and I only see

Chris. Without hesitation I smile back and my body shakes with a painful release. Once

I let go of the grip I have on myself, I feel myself drift off.

"Ruthie let's play a game."

"What you want to play?"

"You pick, you always pick good games."

"Okay, let me think." I paused and sat up straight in the bed. "Okay, okay, let's

play I'm going on a picnic."

"Okay, let me go first. I'm going on a picnic and I'm taking apples."

"I'm going on a picnic and I'm taking bananas and apples."

"I'm going on a picnic and I'm taking cucumbers, bananas and apples."

"I'm going on a—"

"There go daddy, shut up."

We laid flat in the bed and closed our eyes as if we had been sleep the entire

time.

"Ruthie get in here."

My eyes darted open. I inched out of the bed and allowed my feet to scrape the

dusty floor. I glanced back at Sheila still lying underneath the covers. How I hated her

for never getting in trouble and for having such a wonderful relationship with my dad.

As I stood watching Sheila pretend to be sleep I heard my name called once again.

"Yes sir, I'm coming."

Sheila opened her eyes this time and squinted her mouth as if to say sorry for you not being me. I turned toward the door and followed the light flashing from the television. As I walked down the hall I rubbed my fingers across the beige walls. They shivered slightly and my head hung low as I got closer to the living room.

"Ruthie na what I told you about playing at night when I done told you to go to bed. I told you tonight that if I catch you playing and you got to get up early in the morning I was going to whoop yo behind. Don't you member me saying that?"

"Yes sir but it wasn't my fault, Sheila wanted—"

"Now don't you go blaming Sheila. You the oldest and need to be more responsible and I done told you bout that anyway. And since you don't seem to listen to me, I just got to show you that what I say goes."

"But daddy."

"But nothing. Come here."

I jump up and feel the sweat pouring off my forehead. I press my hand into the bed and it's wet too. I quickly take off my silk gown and then plop back down on the sheets with my eyes wide open. I've been having this dream since forever. And what makes it so bad is that it's always the same. It always starts the same, with Sheila and me playing in this same bed. Then my dad would call me out the room cause I was about to get in trouble. I don't know why but this is the farthest I've ever gotten. Usually I never see my dad's face. But today I saw him. And what I saw was scary. He looked indifferent about something. His expression was more of fear than anything else. Maybe like he didn't want to hurt me but also like he was disgusted. I couldn't tell if he was disgusted with me or with himself. He never truly looked me in my eyes. His eyes just sort of shifted back and forth like he couldn't bear the sight of me.

"Ruthie, you up."

He startles the hell out of me. I jump up, grab my housecoat and wrap it around my body. "Yeah daddy but just one minute."

"Whenever you ready. I can wait."

"Oh no, I'm ready, come on in."

He opens the door slowly and peeps in before walking into the room.

"Ah, I didn't mean to make you get up and have to put on something, I just wanted to talk to you before we got ourselves ready to leave."

"What is it daddy? Is something wrong?"

"No ain't nothing wrong I really just wanted to know when you was leaving to go back to Philadelphia."

"Well daddy I'm not sure exactly when I'm leaving. I mean I did want to stay long enough to make sure Sheila was okay."

"Yeah, I understand that."

"But, I do still have a job that I must return to at some point. I have sick days accumulated but I still have a life up there. And I really have a lot to do, you know."

"Of course I do. It's just been so nice having you here and all. You know, I ain't had no company in this here house since, well since yo momma passed away and Sheila got married. So it feels good to have you back."

I can't respond. I sit and stare at him. I feel shocked at him saying that he's enjoyed me cause he sure hasn't acted like it. He barely even talks to me. I'm trying to think of words to say cause I feel like this the right time to get things off my chest. I don't know where to begin but I feel my mouth open.

"Well daddy, I have a question."

"Go head. You can ask me anything."

"Well, I hope you don't think I'm being disrespectful but I don't feel like you care bout me and you never have. You never call me and you ain't hardly said one word to me since I been here. Why don't you like me? I've always loved you and wanted to please you but for some reason that wasn't enough."

I feel myself crying but I let the tears fall and wait for his answer.

"Ruthie, I know I been hard on you. But there are reasons for that. You wouldn't understand even if I wanted you too."

"I'm a grown woman now dad, try me."

"Well, I really don't know how to say it."

"Just say it."

"Ruthie, this something that shoulda been said long time ago. I love you and always have, don't ever forget that. I just didn't know how to handle you. You were so pretty and sweet and gentle. Nothing like me. I was jealous of you. From day one. Yo momma was always playing wit you and babying you up. She loved you more than anything else and I couldn't understand why."

"What you mean, you couldn't understand why a mother would love her daughter? What kind of—"

"It wasn't that. Listen Ruthie, Annabelle never wanted me to tell you but I got to. You ain't my child."

I almost stop breathing.

"What did you just say?"

"I know it's a shock but you ain't really mine. Yo real daddy named Gregory."

"Wait, wait a minute. You mean to tell me you ain't really my daddy. That some man name Gregory really my daddy. And that's the reason you mad at me."

"Ruthie you don't understand. I loved yo momma more than my own life. She was the world to me but when she had you I couldn't handle it cause I knew you wasn't mine. From the moment I saw you I could tell. See yo momma was...she was raped...and when she found out she was pregnant, we wanted it to be mine but when you was born I could tell. I looked at you and you looked more like him than he did. I couldn't handle that. I couldn't look at you without feeling miserable and sad. I—"

The phone starts to ring. We both stare at each other. My dad turns away just as his eyes have started to water. I can't believe what he just told me. I feel nauseous. I think I hear him say my name. I try to ignore it and think about what he's said.

"Ruthie. Phone."

I jump up and run into the kitchen.

"Who is it?"

"A man."

I grab the phone and hear Chris's voice on the other end.

"I'll call you back, okay."

"No, you might as well gone and talk to him. I'm gonna go on over and help James get straight."

He quickly walks out the door but I don't have the strength to protest. I hold the phone to my ear but still without saying anything. After about a minute I exhale and say "Hello." Chris talks as if nothings wrong. But how can he know. How can he know that my daddy ain't really mine and that my momma was raped? Who knows who my real daddy is? What kind of daddy rapes a woman? And why does he have to be my daddy? Maybe John was just saying stuff to hurt me. But he wouldn't lie about something like this, would he? Maybe they think I'm this other man's child cause of what happened but they don't really know.

I listen to Chris ramble on about us but I don't pay him any attention. I finally say that I've got to go and hurry off the phone. I quickly put the phone on the receiver and slide down the wall until my butt feels the floor and relaxes. I don't move for the next hour.

Shelia

Nov. 30, 1976

When I got home the other day I was real surprised. James picked me up that afternoon and when we pulled up into the driveway I felt weird. I guess it was cause I had just got let out of the crazy house and now I had to go home and face whatever it was that made me go fool in the first place. I don't know but it's something about going home after having a nervous breakdown. The doctors didn't really say how bad it was to me but I know it was pretty bad. I mean I felt like it was and I know that everybody probably thought the same thing. I know I ain't crazy. I just can't handle things like most people can. I have to be just a little more patient and a little more calm. I have to start taking my time more. The doctor's told me to just stop and think things through if I have too. To be afraid. Ain't nothing wrong with that. I just felt the pressure and couldn't stop it from blowing up in my face. That's alright cause I got myself straight now.

Anyway back to what happened when I got home. Well, when I walked in the house everyone jumped out and said SURPRISE. I was real shocked. I couldn't believe James had got my family and friends together to see me after I had been acting like a damn fool. I was just so happy. The first face I saw was Ruthie. She looked herself but still a little sad. It was okay cause I was just so happy to see her face. No matter how confused and upset she seemed. Then was my daddy. He gave me a big hug which is kinda strange for him cause he barely came to see me the whole time I was in the nut house. He checked in wit James but I just thought he was so disappointed in me that he couldn't bear to look at me. But he looked at me anyway. He seemed to watch me closely, he even watched Ruthie too. Kinda stared at us. Sometimes I thought he looked at Ruthie more. Like he had something he needed to tell her but couldn't find a way to get it out. I don't know but maybe he was finally gonna stop being so tuff on her. After that I saw my friend Carla and then Hattie and then Dee (that's what we call her) and Ruby. These were the people I usually hung out wit and some of them well maybe all of them I would call my best friends. We did everything together. Drank on the weekends, tried smoking reffa together, hung out at the juke joint together. Everything. Everybody else was just faces from church and around town who came to be nosy. I didn't care cause for a few hours I felt like I had a little bit of peace. That was the first time in a long time I felt like I didn't have a care in the world.

James

I GET ONE drink. Just a little bit of Gin and juice that I have left over from the other night. I think things went good. Everybody seemed to enjoy themselves. Sheila was happy, I think. I still feel a little funny from the other night and I think she can tell something's wrong. I can't even go back in the bedroom till I take this drink. Just this one to calm my nerves. I been waiting on this night for the longest time. See right after the party we both were tired so we fell asleep and then last night I was extra busy at the shop so Sheila was sleep when I got home but tonight's the night. She seems sort of different. I mean the whole way back home I was searching for something to say. We didn't say much but I can tell she was happy when she came home. When everybody jumped out and welcomed her home, Sheila just looked at me and her eyes got real bright like and she looked happy. I hope she looks that happy when I go back in the bedroom. She said she was gonna go take a bath and then she wanted to talk to me. Maybe I ought to take two drinks since she said she got to talk to me. Yeah, just one more drink. I should walk on outside and take a smoke too. Na, I better just wait on the smoke till after she say what she gotta say. Yeah, I'll wait to do that but I will have one more drink.

I swallow the last of the alcohol and stand up. I stretch my arms out and start walking down the hall. I look in the room and see Sheila dozing off. I slip out of my clothes and try to get in the bed without waking her up.

"Hey baby, you finally came to bed."

"Yeah, I was just trying to straighten up a little for I got ready for bed."

"You know I really enjoyed the party. Thank you."

"You're welcome. You know I love you and would do anything for you so I just wanted you to know that. That's one reason I had the party. Sheila I'm gone do better. I promise."

"I know. We both got to do better. We both got to give a little more."

"I know. So what did you want to talk to me bout?"

"Well James I been doing a lot of thinking since I been at the hospital."

Sheila shifts her body and looks me straight in the eyes.

"James we got another chance at this. We really do. I coulda been dead and gone. It scares me to think I coulda killed myself."

I sit up too.

"Sheila you scared me too. I can't imagine you hurting yourself. I definitely can't imagine you not being here. Please don't ever do me like that again."

"I won't. I promise."

"Good," I say as I kiss her on the forehead.

"But listen, you can't keep doing everything you been. I need you here with me. I can't handle all the nights out without you calling to say if you living and okay. Or when you drink all the time and come in here and want to fuss wit me. I can't do it no more. My mind ain't strong enough and frankly I'm tired. Tired of crying at night cause you ain't here. I'm sick of walking around on eggshells around you when you been out drinking and smoking. And I'm damn sure sick of hearing bout every other woman that you round here sleeping wit. That's so disrespectful. Shit you don't hear bout me in the streets do you?"

"No."

"Well, I shouldn't hear bout you. And definitely not wit no other women. Do you know how that makes me feel? It makes me feel like I'm not good enough and that I don't measure up to you. Maybe you don't get turned on by me no more."

"Listen, it ain't got nothing to do with you. It's been me the whole time. I'm the one who got the problem. And it ain't really even a problem. Don't none of those women mean nothing to me. As a matter of fact I'm through wit that. I promise. And don't you dare think you don't satisfy me. You do more than enough. I just been down and out lately. And I haven't really found a way to deal wit what all we done lost. I still ain't really let it all sink in cause I haven't wanted to accept it. But every since you did that stuff, it woke me up. It made me realize that I need you and don't know what kind of life I'd have without you. You back in my life now and I wouldn't do nothing to mess that up."

"Well, I'm glad to hear all that but you got to show me. Saying all this don't mean shit if you ain't doing it. Now I don't mean to sound like I don't care no more but the fact is, I don't. If I keep hearing this same thang and you keep doing the same thang, you gots to go. I mean that. And as much as it would hurt me to put you out and be by myself, I'll do it. I got to start thinking about me and appreciating myself more. So I'm serious. From now on things gone change. Or. Or else we can't be together."

"Okay. I understand completely. And I'll show you. I will."

"Now that that's been said, did you miss me?"

"Of course I missed you. It was hard for me to even sleep in this bed without you being by my side."

"Well, I'm here now and mighty glad to be back in my own bed."

"I'm glad to have you back."

"Just one more thing."

Sheila gets up and sits on my lap with her body facing me. I wrap my arms around her backside.

"What's up?"

"I'm pregnant again."

For a while I just look at her. I really can't say nothing. I'm happy, but I'm scared. Scared to death to try to have another child. I'm still looking at her.

"You don't have nothing to say."

"I'm scared."

"Me too. But I'm happy."

"Are you really?"

"Of course I'm happy. Why wouldn't I be?"

"I don't know I just was a little afraid that you wouldn't be happy bout it, being that we done went through so much."

"I don't care. This time things gone be different and I know that. I believe we gone have a healthy baby and as a matter fact I'm gonna make it work."

Sheila smiles hard at me and then she kisses me on the lips. She then slides down, wraps her arms around my body, and hides her head within my chest.

"Thank you," I whisper as my head automatically tilts toward the sky.

John

"**I FINALLY TOLD** Ruthie the truth. I told her that I wasn't her father. I been carrying that weight since she was born."

"Well I don't think you should beat yourself up over it. You did the right thing. You found the courage to tell her the truth and now you both can move on."

"But Edna you don't understand. You shoulda seen her face. She looked crushed. Looked like I had just pulled her heart out her body and put it in her hands. She just looked at me. Looked at me like every bit of pain you can imagine was felt at that very moment and I know it's all my fault."

Edna put her hands on mine.

"And now look at me. I'm sitting here in your house cause I can't go back home. I'm scared to face my own daughter. It was so funny at the party. We walked in together but that was it. She couldn't even look at me."

"John stop blaming yourself. You can't help what yo wife did back when y'all was together. I'm surprised you still was wit her."

"Don't talk bout Annabelle like that. It's a lot you don't know bout what happened between us. So don't go blaming her."

"Well I'm sorry but I just don't understand why you always got to be defending her. You act like she some sort of saint or something. You act like she just didn't sleep wit no other man. That's the reason y'all in this mess now."

"Hush Edna. I don't want to hear you talk like that no more. Don't say nothing bout Annabelle. Nothing and I mean it. You wouldn't understand, so let's just forget it."

"John listen. Me and you been sneaking round trying to see each other for years now. You ain't never introduced me to yo children and it don't seem like you making no attempt to do so but I still love you. I love you cause you a good man. Yeah I wish you would let me be a part of your family but I ain't gone pressure you. But this, this something I need to know. I don't care what you did in yo past. All I know is, I care so much for you and want to know bout you and what make you cry and laugh and smile. I've always wanted to know these things. I've always wanted to be close enough to you that you could tell me anything. So now I guess I'm asking you to let me be that person. Let me be close to you and love you. Please. Tell me what you been hiding for all these years."

I simply look at this woman. Just look into her eyes and see how sincere she is. She's honest and concerned and she's right, for years I've been doing this to her. But she don't understand. I loved Annabelle with all my heart and soul. I feel like I still owe her. Like she's never completely forgiven me. Even after being dead and gone I still can't let go. Still don't know how to let the past stay there in the past. And now this woman asking me to forgive myself and move on. Whether Annabelle done forgave me or not it's time for me to move on. I want to. I want to make her understand everything so maybe she'll be able to accept me and accept everything bout me but I don't know if I can.

"John, I'm talking to you."

"I'm sorry Edna, my mind went somewhere else."

"As usual."

"Okay you want to hear it, then I'll tell you. The whole nasty ugly story bout why Ruthie ain't mine. Maybe you'll leave Annabelle lone now and understand that this all my fault. I'm the one who let this happen....'' My voice fades off as my mind rewinds many years backward. Back to when everything that was good suddenly went bad.

"It happened a few years after we were married. We were happy. Nothing seemed to matter to us cept for each other. We worked and then we went home and cuddled and talked and laughed. It was the same routine everyday. Not so much the routine but the work. The work was what was killing us. Breaking down our spirits. And not to mention our boss. His name was Gregory. He was a white man who seemed like he hated me. He made me work extra hours just so he could talk to Annabelle. Just so he could have extra time to make her clean his house or bake a cake or anything just to keep her from me. There wasn't nothing I could do so I just let him keep me working and slaving for him til one night.

"I left the fields at sundown even though I was posed to stay a lil longer. I was tired. I had been working extra hours all week and then getting up at sunup and by that time I was just feed up. I was sick of the cotton and the sun beating me on my back everyday. I was feed up with the blisters on my hands. Well anyway, I left the fields at around 7 o'clock that night and walked bout a mile to my friend Larry's house. I had a cup of creek liquor and then I walked on back down the road home. I always did hate myself for being selfish and wasting time drinking wit Larry but I needed it. I needed to relieve my mind and let off some stress. So, I sat wit Larry and drank a little bit and joked around and shot the breeze till maybe sometime past 9, maybe even 10. After that I walked home and when I got to the step the door was cracked. That was strange cause Annabelle always closed the door. She was nothing like me. I never locked the door, still don't except for at night. Well, I walked in and called her name. I didn't hear nothing. I looked around and saw that the biscuits were waiting to be put in the oven so I figured maybe Annabelle had fell asleep waiting on me. I got down the hall and peeked in the room."

I pause and look up at Edna.

"Keep going."

"Well. What I saw is always gone be in my mind. I remember the expression on her face in my mind like it just happened. Sometimes I go to bed and dream about it. Her face just stares at me. Asking me why I let it happen to her.

"So when I looked at her face she looked up at mine. Time she looked at me she looked right back down and grabbed her knees. Like she couldn't stand to look at me. Like she didn't want me to see her like that. But I looked at her anyway and looked at the man lying on the floor beside her. He had a gash on his forehead that was bleeding, He was out cold. Apparently Annabelle had done it. She did what I was scared to do. Defend herself. I knew long ago that Greg had his eyes on my woman but did I care. No. I cared but I wasn't man enough to protect what was mine. I was so afraid of this man that I let him come in my house, while I was out doing his work and allowed him to

rape my wife. He sat there while I was out drinking wit my buddy and forced himself on

Annabelle. I knew he wanted her way before it happened but I didn't want that to be

true. I didn't want him to be capable of such a thing but I knew that's what he wanted.

Knew it for a long time but I let him keep me sweating in the hot sun while he tried to get

close to Annabelle.

"I just felt so pitiful. So mad. So angry. It was amazing how many different

things I felt at the same time. And the thing that make it bad is that I didn't even kill this

man. I wanted to but... Truth is I was scared. I know Annabelle expected me to get him

for what he did to her but I couldn't. He had raped my wife and I didn't even hit him or

punch him or stomp him. I just looked. Watched as the blood flowed down Annabelle's

leg. Watched her as she sat there with her head hung low as if she was the one to blame.

Watched her later have the same nervous breakdown that Sheila just had. Like she was

ashamed of what happened. Like it was her fault. But I wanted to tell her it wasn't her

fault. That it was all my fault but I didn't. I didn't even say that I felt guilty. I couldn't.

My pride wouldn't let me. Ain't that something? That's how valuable I felt. That my

pride was all I had and that it was worth more than making my wife feel like she wasn't

the blame for somebody else taking advantage of her. That's why I'm the blame for this.

I'm the reason I don't have a good relationship wit Ruthie. I could never look at her.

Annabelle found out she was pregnant a few weeks after everything happened and I knew

it wasn't mine. There was no doubt in my mind that she was going to be having his baby.

And I couldn't accept that. No I wouldn't accept it. And Ruthie came out looking just

like him. I didn't even stay there after I saw her face. Didn't even look at Ruthie. Funny thing is we never talked bout it. We swept it under the rug like it didn't even happen. Like Ruthie was mine and that was it.

"And as Annabelle sat there grabbing her knees, I went over to her and tried to touch her. Just wipe the tears off her face but she jumped. Like she was scared to death. Scared of me. I just sat there beside her and held her for a while. I didn't even clean her up then. When we saw Gregory start to stir like he might wake up, I kissed Annabelle's forehead and then picked her up and took her to her momma's house. I walked bout 2 miles wit her in my arms. She had her arms wrapped around me and I was walking and crying. No talking just crying. Not only for her but more for me. I was selfish. How could I face people? How could I explain to her momma what had happened? How could I face Gregory after that day? And believe me it took everything I had to stand there and listen to him tell his buddies and wife that an old mule kicked him in the face which explained where he got that black eye and knot on the side of his head. You'll never understand how I felt listening to him but not saying anything to prove he was a liar. I couldn't, cause who would have believed me. Who would have believed that this white man wanted my wife so bad that he had to rape her just to get her? Who would have believed that he wanted this woman who was as dark as night? Nobody. Nobody would have even considered any of this so I kept my mouth closed. Didn't even speak his name again until I said it the other day."

By this time Edna just standing looking at me shaking her head. I can't believe I just told her everything. All about Annabelle and what happened that messed everything up. I wonder what she thinking. I know she think I'm selfish and now she probably

won't talk to me no more, but I only gave her what she asked for. The truth.

"Where you going?"

She doesn't answer.

"See I told you this was too much for you to handle. I told you."

She stops dead in her tracks and turns around.

"What makes you think that?"

"Well you the one who walking away."

"John I'm going to get some tissue so I can blow my nose."

"Oh."

She goes to the bathroom and comes out with a handful of tissue that she hands

to me. I didn't even realize I was crying too.

"John this isn't going to scare me away. You're right you were selfish. But at

the same time I can understand. I can understand where you're coming from. You were

hurt, confused, and angry. No one can blame you for that. And it wasn't your fault. You

were caught in the middle. You've got to believe that this situation wasn't because of

you."

I don't say nothing. I stand near the recliner looking down at the floor. Staring

at one piece of paper that's been here since I don't know how long. It's the same piece of

paper or lent or whatever that I been dying to pick up but just don't have the strength to

bend down and get. That piece of trash that's probably just gonna stay there till

somebody comes and moves it with they feet while they walk and then it'll just be put

somewhere else for people to walk over and never pick up. I stand here almost daydreaming about the tiny piece of trash that's on the floor when I feel Edna's presence. She's standing in front of me. I don't look up until she lifts my head with her fingers. I'm already taller than her so when she lifts my head, I can see straight down into the top of her graying roots.

"John I understand. I may not agree with everything but I understand. Now you can move on. I love you no matter what and this isn't going to change the way I feel about you. It was a complicated situation so it's nobody's fault except for Gregory. And the fact that you and Ruthie don't get along is understandable too. Trust me, who knows how some other man would have handled the situation. I think you're a good man cause what other man do you know would have raised a child that he knew wasn't his and provide for her as if she were his own flesh and blood. I admire you for what you did. John, you have nothing to be ashamed of."

I grab Edna in my arms and we embrace and rock back and forth on top of the small piece of lent. We stop hugging and I look her in the face.

"What's wrong now?"

"There's more."

Ruthie

I CAN'T BELIEVE that Chris gone let me ride in a damn taxi to get home. I know that me not talking to him while I was home has a lot to do with everything but does that mean you treat me like shit. The damn cabdriver stinks and he's smoking. Chris knows good and damn well I can't tolerate no smoke. He knows that. I don't give a damn what kind of meeting he had at his job or what he had to do. I need him. I need to talk to someone about my problems. About how my daddy done dropped a damn bomb on me. He basically destroyed everything I knew to be true all my life. I have so many questions. Like why did it take him bout 30 years to tell me? Didn't anyone think I needed to know who my biological father was or that he was a rapist and whatever else? I just can't quite understand what's going on. And of course my dad wouldn't even tell me anything else. It's so frustrating cause he stayed gone practically the entire time I was home. Went over to some woman named Edna's house. Claims she some friend that needed his help. Like I'm some kind of damn fool or something. But for all these years I have been a fool. A fool bout who I was and who I belonged too. I've always felt like something was wrong. Always felt like maybe I was out of place. I knew I didn't look nothing like my daddy but I guess after years of being in his presence I just started to resemble him a little. It feels like everything I know to be true, isn't. Sheila's only my half sister, even though I shouldn't feel like that. Does she know? If so how long has she known and kept this from me? And now what about my real daddy? Is he alive? Does he know he has a daughter, who according to my father, looks just like him? I wish I knew. I wish I knew what to do or say. All I do know is that I've got a lot to figure out.

Oh, and note to self, kick Chris's ass to the curb as soon as I get in the door.

I give the taxi driver a ten-dollar bill and before I know it he takes off with my change. I don't care if it was only two dollars. See that's exactly why I hate these motherfuckers. Exactly why. I get my suitcase off the ground and struggle to get it up the two flights of stairs. Once I get to my door, I pull out my house key and put it in the lock. When I open the door I almost jump back outside.

"Hey baby."

"Chris what the hell are you doing here?"

"Is that anyway to greet a man who is sitting here with candles set up all around the house and with your favorite meal cooked and waiting on you."

"Chris I don't know what to say."

"Don't say anything, just come in here and act like you're happy to see me."

I walk in, drop my bags on the floor and give Chris a big hug.

"Maybe you are a little happy to see me."

I smile at him and then peck him on the lips.

"Alright maybe you're getting a little happier by the minute.

"So this is why you made me take a cab to get back home."

He laughs.

"Well actually I was going to come get you but I did have some business to take care of."

"And what kind of business could be more important that coming to pick your woman up from the train station instead of making her sit in a cab while the taxi driver blows smoke in her face and then leaves without giving her change."

"This kind of business."

Chris immediately gets on his knee and pulls a black box out his pocket. He stares into my eyes and blows a kiss towards me.

"Ruthie. I love you. I know we've been down this road before about being together and allowing ourselves to trust each other but I think it's time. There's no one else I'd rather be with. Nobody else that makes me feel the way you do. Nobody else I would rather lay next to every night. And nobody else I want to have my children. I love you and want you to be with me for the rest of our lives. I know you weren't expecting this but while you were gone I missed you so much. I looked at your picture everyday and just counted the days until I knew you were coming home. I need you in my life. I don't care how long we've been physically knowing each other, I feel like I've known you much longer. Please say yes. Please say yes, you'll marry me."

I stand in front of this beautiful man, crying happy tears. He's right I never would have guessed it. This was the furthest thing on my mind, although I have thought about the type of husband he would be. The type of man he would really make me and I like it. I like what I've seen of him. But what I haven't seen is the problem. That's what scares me. The waking up every single morning to the same face. The way he leaves his dirty socks on the floor for days without picking them up and I finally get tired of them staring at me and pick them up myself. Or the way he pees and never lets down the seat. I always go in there at night and fall in. No matter how much I say, "let down the seat," he still leaves it up. I don't know if I can handle that. I don't know if I can handle the fact that he works overtime a lot. Maybe I'm not the marrying type cause I'm sure I'll have to deal with these things with anyone else, but am I ready to deal with these things with him? I sure hope so, cause alone is a lonely place. And I know if I say no, that's exactly where I'll be. Alone and feeling mighty lonely.

I look down into Chris's face and see him getting a little impatient. He hasn't said anything but I can tell. He's still kneeling. Still looking up at me, hoping I'll say yes. I gently rub his hair. He has such pretty hair. It's wavy and soft. I rub is hair more then kneel down with him.

"Chris, I really didn't think you would say anything like this to me. Actually, I said I wasn't going to have anything to do with you anymore just because you didn't pick me up. But I was being selfish. And I definitely don't deserve you. But since you're here and I love you more than anything else I've known our loved besides my momma and sister, I will marry you. I will be your wife."

Chris's face lights up. He grabs me in his arms and we hug and kiss for the longest time. I can't even remember how we get to the bedroom but all I do know is that he's making me feel like I'm tied up in him somehow. It seems like I'm connecting to him at this very moment.

I guess it's around nine in the morning and I'm just turning over. I feel my stomach aching cause I needed to use the bathroom half the night but was too lazy to get up. I move the covers back and slip out of bed. I quickly walk out the room and down

the hall into the bathroom. I sit on the toilet and let the water flow out. I must have held

that for a long time cause I been peeing for like two or three minutes straight. After the

last little bit trickles out I wipe and stand up. Sleeping naked sure does help when you

got to go to the bathroom. I flush, wash my hands and run through the cold apartment. I

slow down when I get back in the room because Chris is still sleep and I don't want to

wake him. Once I ease back into bed I look over at Chris. He's snoring lightly. I watch

him carefully and notice that his left leg jumps a little as if he's having a bad dream or

something. I study how his skin looks and the way his mouth stays wide open if he's

laying on his back the way he's doing now. These are small things I've never noticed

before but that I can't imagine not seeing now. I can't believe he asked me to marry him.

Somehow I feel like this is God answering my prayers. Like He finally heard enough of

my cries and decided that now it's time to let me have something good and real. I take

the tips of my fingers and rub Chris on the face. He moves a little and then turns on his

side. He mumbles something under his breathe too. I smile cause I think it's cute how he

sleeps.

Finally, I position myself behind his body and wrap my arms around him. I hold

on tight. It's been so long since I felt like I wasn't alone. Just as I think about being by

myself Chris grabs my arm with his hand as if to hold me closer. I cuddle behind him

and dream about us.

Shelia

Feb. 27, 1977

So far so good. Me and James been doing good. I can't complain one bit, except for now. It's only 12:00 but it's not like him to be out this late. But other than today he stays here wit me all the time and make sure I'm fine. We haven't had no arguments lately and we just get along fine now. It's like he's a new man. He acts like he geniuenly cares bout whether or not the baby make it into the world. I can't complain one bit. Sometimes he do too much. Like at night he'll tuck me in and kiss me on the forehead before I go to sleep. Especially if I'm real sleepy. He'll even go to the store and get me something to eat if what I want ain't in the refrigerater. I'm so happy. He makes me feel so good. Like how he treated me when I first met him and he first started courting me. We doing so good. But the real reason I'm writing tonight since it been so long is that Ruthie called me last night. She called to let me know how everything was going up her way, about her engagement, which is still a shock to me, but then she started asking me questions. First she started telling me about this dream she done had and how it keep coming back. She even asked me if I remember the night she was talking about. I told her no. But truth is I do and it seems like she think I know what happened too. I member it like it was yesterday. We was in the bed playing. We knew we was supposed to be sleep cause daddy told us to go to bed and to not be playing. Everything in that night happened so fast. See momma wasn't there to save Ruthie from daddy. It make me sad to think of what really went on. I mean it wasn't nothing I could do. I was just a child myself. But daddy didn't have to do what he did. He called Ruthie out the room. I don't know if it was her who was talking then but I was the one who heard him. He was coming down the hall, stomping. He has heavy feet. I told Ruthie to shut up. I wish she woulda shut up a little sooner. Anyway, he beat Ruthie till she passed out. I saw him. But he didn't see me till the end. I member helping Ruthie up and taking her in the bathroom and washing her up. She was bleeding and it was like he was trying to kill her. Like he was mad at her for more than just talking and not listening to him. I never quite understood all that happened but he told me to keep his secret and till this day nobody knows what I saw. Not even momma. I never wanted to make her upset. Ruthie didn't remember. She knew something happened but I acted like I was sleep so she don't even know that I had to clean her body that night. She musta just blocked everything out her mind or something. All I know is to this day I don't want to bring up the past but if she keep asking me bout it I'm probably gonna have to come clean bout what I know happened that night. The truth about what happened.

Now where the hell James at. It's 12:45 and he still ain't here. I know he a changed man. He got to be. We done been doing real good these past few months so for him to go back on all that is crazy. He left round 8 or 9 but maybe he wit Charlie and I know how they get when they drinking and stuff. But he at least could have called. He could stop what he doing for 5 minutes to say let me tell Sheila where I'm at. Sometimes he just don't think.

Damnit it's almost 2 and he still ain't here. We been back together for about 3 months without any problems and now he go and pull this. He must be tired of me already. But the doctor's told me not to worry bout stuff I can't control. But I just can't. I don't know what to do. I love him so much. But for the life of me he just won't do right. All I want is for us to have this baby. What happened last time I try to forget about but I still feel bad about it. If there was one thing that I did wrong was that I did too much worrying. And I promised myself and the Lord that if I ever got another chance to have a child I wouldn't worry no matter what but look at me, I'm sitting here crying bout to have a fit cause James ain't here yet.

Well, it's a little after 2 now and I hear the car pulling up.

James

ME AND SHEILA didn't say nothing when I walked in last night. I know she disappointed but this time it ain't my fault. I swear it. I just had to do it. Had to go see Mae. Sheila wasn't gone understand so I didn't feel like it was no need to tell her nothing bout it. So when I walked in last night, I got out of my clothes and got in the bed. I know she was up cause she moved on her side as soon as I walked in the room. I guess she must still be mad cause she ain't said hardly two words to me this morning. And I know the ride to work ain't gone be no different. She keeps walking past me while we both trying to be in the bathroom at the same time and she hardly even look at me. She looks straight ahead. We both standing in the bathroom, me trying to put on my clothes and her putting on makeup so I know she itching to say something. Well I know I ain't gone say nothing cause I don't want to start no argument.

"So James did you have a good time last night?"

Here she go.

"Listen Sheila, don't start okay. There was nothing to my night. I went had a few drinks and that was it. I ain't been out in a long time so what's wrong wit that."

"Ain't nothing wrong wit that but you coulda at least called."

"You know what you right, I shoulda called and tried not to loose track of time but I did and I'm sorry."

"Well when are you gonna stop saying sorry and start doing."

I really don't feel like this today cause I got enough to worry bout so why she got to keep going. I'm just gonna shut up and walk on back in the room.

"So where you going? Am I getting on your nerves?"

"Yes you are. You already made your point so why the fuck you got to drill it in the ground. I really don't feel like fussing today okay."

"Fine."

"Fine."

Good she shuts up.

"Sheila you bout ready cause I got to clean up the shop today."

I'm ready, just wait a minute."

"Well, I'll be waiting in the car."

I go outside, light a cigarette and stand on the porch. This how she do. If she don't get her way or if she feel like I'm rushing her, she'll take her sweet ass time to do something. So she gone be late for work cause she mad at me.

I keep puffing on my cigarette and once I finish I hear her coming. I crank up the car and pat the gas a few times before she gets outside. We ride in complete silence. I don't turn on the radio cause she said she don't want to hear nothing. When I get her to her job she don't even say bye. She just gets out the car and I see her disappear in the hall. I sit there in the car and look around for a few minutes before another car horn knocks me out of my funk and I move forward. I don't bother turning on the radio cause

I'm tired and cranky and really don't want to hear the noise either. I drive to 1824 Market Street, park in the dirt lot and walk in my two-room building. When I open the door the shop looks a mess. The floor has hair spread everywhere and the chairs aren't in the proper order and it's some smashed glass on the floor. I look around and shake my head. All because I was mad and confused last night, I almost destroyed one of the few things I can call my own. I couldn't help it. I had to know. Just had to know if what Charlie told me was true. I had already broke it off wit her but I needed the truth, so I went to see Mae.

Before I even got out the car good the door flew open.

"Hey baby, what's up? I just got here and I really need to talk to—"

"I know. I heard you drive up. So what you want tonight?"

"Listen, I need to talk to you bout us?"

"Well what. I mean is you trying to be wit me permanently? Is you?"

"Woman, I'm married. What kind of question is that? And besides I think it's time for us to just end this anyway."

"That's fucked up, you bastard," Mae said as she ran towards me with her fist balled up and her arms swinging in a circle.

I grabbed her and shook her until she stopped hitting at me. She started crying in my arms until I let go and she fell on the ground.

"Woman what the hell wrong wit you. I don't have time for this shit. You knew I had a wife and it's important now that I leave you alone. I don't love you, I love her and always will."

Mae just sat down in the red dirt digging her fingernails deep into the clay. Then without anything funny being said, she started laughing. She started giggling harder and harder. The laughing almost got out of control, so I just stomped my foot in the ground, and watched a dusty cloud come up round my legs.

"You crazy. I knew I shouldn't—"

"Shouldn't what...shouldn't na got me pregnant. Now that's what you shouldn't na did. See," Mae said as she pointed to her stomach.

"Yeah that's right I'm round five months."

I looked at her. Looked at her real hard and saw that she did have a pouch where she didn't used to have one. I stared even harder and saw that she looks sorta, maybe a little bigger than Sheila does and Sheila bout four months now. I really couldn't tell wit her clothes on but she lifted up her shirt so I would be sure. I couldn't say nothing cause even though I know she said she was pregnant and even though I saw that she was pregnant, she couldn't be. Not now.

"Mae what the hell you talking about. You said that you couldn't get pregnant and now you saying you bout to have my baby. Shit, I don't know who else you been fucking wit, so don't think you gon' blame that shit on me."

Mae slowly stood up and walked towards me.

"It figures you would say something like that."

"What the hell was I thinking," I said to myself as I paced back and forth in front of the porch. "Well you know what you got to do right."

"Huh?"

"You heard me. Get rid of it."

Mae's head dropped, as she tried to understand my words.

"You mean to tell me you expect me to get rid of this precious child just cause yo wife pregnant too. I can't believe you would even ask me some shit like that."

"Well, whatever. I'm not claiming it cause I don't know who the fuck you done been wit."

"I'm sitting here telling you that I ain't been wit nobody else."

"Well everybody know you a lying whore so I don't know what I was thinking in the first place."

Mae looked me in the eyes. I knew she wasn't that type of woman to be sleeping round but I didn't know what else to say. I just stood there and looked down at the ground before I was able look her in the face. She was scared but her eyes looked like she was more hurt. Hurt that I could say that to her knowing full well she was only giving it up to me. Out of nowhere she runs towards me. She stood so close to me, I could feel her breathe on my lips. Without saying anything she slapped me in the face. Before I knew it I had picked up her up by the neck and was choking her. Her feet where dangling off the ground and the only thing I could think about was Vietnam.

Pow, Pow.

"Oh shit, they coming, man run. Come on James snap out of it man, those shots they firing. Run."

Roscoe, my Vietnam buddy slapped me, to wake me from my frozen state. As soon as Roscoe's hand hit my face, I grabbed his neck and began to choke him.

"Boom."

Somehow I just dropped Mae from my hands and she landed on the hard ground. I heard her coughing, and yelling. I'm sure she was crying too.

"Do you think you can just leave me and yo baby? You must be crazy! I'm gonna tell Sheila anyway, she gone know that since she can't have yo baby, I will," Mae said as she reached toward the leg of my pants.

I looked in her direction, shook my head, kicked her off me and then walked to the car. "What have I done," was all I could say while I beat myself in the head. I didn't even look back to see if she was okay. Simply got in my car and drove to the shop.

*****

"Hey James man what it look like?"

I don't answer. I hadn't even heard the bell on the door jingle. I simply stare at the poster of a black woman with long hair, a red bikini and a Budweiser in her hand.

"Yeah she fine but damn, she got you in a trance."

"Ah man, what it look like?"

"Shit, I ought to be asking you that same thang, cause you the one who in another world."

"Man, you know how it is."

"Yeah I know how it is but damn."

"Listen Jimmy don't worry bout me. I'm fine, okay."

"Okay, whatever man. Besides I didn't come here to try to figure you out, I came to get a haircut."

"Alrighty then. Sit on down while I get set up."

I walk to the wooden counter and start cleaning my razor and set of clippers. After thoroughly wiping the metal with alcohol, I call Jimmy to come sit in the black chair.

Damn that Jimmy slow. I watch him drag himself over and finally sit down in the chair. Once he seems comfortable enough, I fling the cape in the air and allow it to slowly fall into his lap. Then I wrap a piece of paper-towel around his neck and tightly fasten the cape on top of the thick paper.

"So what ya want it to look like today."

"Just kinda even it up and shape around the edges."

"Okay."

Just as I grab the hand scissors, two more men walk in the shop.

"What's up y'all?"

"Ain't nothing."

"What bout you James, you alright?"

"Yeah man, I cool."

Leroy Fuller was my last customer. Now that he done left the shop, I decide to sweep up before I go back over to the hole. Every since everything happened last night I've been a little stressed. All I need is for Sheila to find out bout what done happened so she can throw me out the house.

I sweep up the last little bit of hair, close up the shop and walk to my car. I really don't want to go out here but I done called the man that gave me the free set the first time. I know I can't be messing wit him like that cause he ain't to be played wit. He done broke a man's legs cause he left him hanging. So I get in the car, crank it and back out the driveway. I take the long route out to *Lucky's*. I need time to think. I ride through town and then drive out towards the funeral home so I can get to the highway. Once I get to Hwy 1, I speed up and take the left. I ride for another 10 minutes before making a right onto this dirt road. A mile down that dirt road and I make another right and here I am pulling into *Lucky's* dirt driveway. I look over at the hole and think about my life. I done dug myself in a hole and now I can't get out of it. And look here I am bout to get further inside.

I look around and out of nowhere I see a tall lanky man dressed in dress slacks and a shirt with a neatly trimmed low cut. He kinda struts towards me as I get out the car. When we meet, we slap hands and exchange money for drugs. It's quick. We don't even say much. Just *what's up?* and *I'll get back at cha later*. After that the man disappears as easy as he came.

Once I get back in the car, I pull open the dingy bag and examine the white stuff that's stuck in one corner of the tiny sack. I decide I'll hold off on smoking it. I throw it in the glove compartment. I pat the gas as I turn the ignition and again I'm off but this time I'm going home. I walk in the door at around 7:00 and see that Sheila's hasn't gotten home yet. There's no food on the stove like normal so I know something's wrong. I walk over to the sink and see chicken that's thawed out and is ready to be cleaned and cooked. She must have been home. I don't think about that too much even though I know it's strange for Sheila to leave and go off without leaving a note or something.

I go to the bathroom, wash my hands, walk back to the kitchen and start cleaning the chicken. Once it's been cleaned and seasoned I get the grease ready so I can start cooking. I put on a pot of rice and open a can of sweet peas. I figure I'd have everything set up nice for Sheila to make up for last night. I better cause I still got to break this news to her. After I put the chicken in the hot grease I put on my Donnie Hathaway eight track. I hear Sheila. I go to the hallway to greet her as she comes in the door.

"Hey baby. Where you been?"

She don't say nothing, she simply looks past me and walks down the hall. After she takes off her shoes, she marches back down the hall until she's standing directly in my face.

"What Sheila, why the hell you in my face like that."

"James, you didn't think I would find out bout you and that Bitch Mae. How could you?"

"What you talking bout?"

"Just like yo black ass to sit there and act like you don't know what I'm talking bout. I saw her today and if I was trying to lose another child I woulda tried to kill her and you too. That bitch came to my job to tell me where you was at last night. But I can't even stress no more. Apparently you don't give a fuck about whether or not this child makes it or not anyway."

"Come on now Sheila you know that I want this child just as much as you and I don't want nothing bad to happen. You got to believe that. But listen Sheila, she didn't

mean nothing. I don't love her, I love you. It was just—"

"What! What can you say to justify fucking some other bitch and you got a wife

and another child on the way, waiting at home. Huh! So that's where you was at last

night, right? You know what don't even answer that. I already know the answer to

that….just how? How could you lay up with some other woman and then come home to

me? I done been through this so much that I don't even know what to do. But now I'm

tired and I can't take it no more. I ain't gone sit here and look like no fool just cause you

want to be wit every woman cept for your own. Do you know how many men want me

and would treat me right."

"I know all these men look at you. You beautiful. But last night I wasn't

sleeping wit Mae. Come on Sheila, I don't feel like fussing over some bullshit that didn't

even mean nothing. That was months ago. That woman lying. Na, I'm sitting here

cooking you a fucking meal and you bitching over some shit that didn't even matter."

"Why should I believe you? I've trusted you in the past and it didn't get me

nowhere. Besides you must be losing yo' motherfucking mind. You think I'm just gone

sit here and let you do whatever you want. And what you cooking got to do wit one

damn thing. I cook every day, the least you could do is cook a goddamn meal. I do it for

you."

"Okay you right, I'm wrong but it was nothing. For real, it was a one-time thing

and that was long time ago."

"Well you know what, it don't even matter cause I'm tired of the bullshit. I'm

tired of you staying out all night long getting drunk and then coming in here like ain't shit wrong. But now that I know where you been going, I want you to get out. Go see Mae, sleep in her bed tonight, cause I don't want to see your face."

"Oh so you putting me out. Fine fuck it. I'll leave."

And as Donnie sings, "whether she knows it or not she really needs me too," I stomp out of the house.

Ruthie

I JUMP UP and let out the loudest scream I've ever made in my life.

"Baby what's wrong?"

"I don't know my stomach's killing me."

"Well you want me to get you something?"

"Just some soda."

As Chris walks out the room I scream again and he runs back in the bedroom.

"Come on, I'm taking you to the hospital."

"No, just go get some ginger ale or Pepsi or something. I'll be fine. Please, just pour me some soda in a cup and bring it here."

He doesn't argue he just goes. I know he's worried cause this is the third time this week I woke up in the middle of the night either screaming from a dream, some sort of pain or stopped him during sex because it hurt too bad. It's beginning to worry me too. I used to have sharp pains in my stomach all the time but never more than once or twice a month. Now it seems like they're coming all too often.

"Here drink this."

I grab the glass and put it to my lips. It didn't take long for me to start sipping on the cool soda and feel it slide down to my insides. Instead of the coolness soothing my stomach, I drop the soda in my lap and curl up in a ball in the bed. This time Chris won't listen to me. He picks me up, runs all the way down two flights of stairs and puts me in the car. We're both practically naked. He did stop long enough to put on some sweat pants, coat and shoes but he takes me as I am. In a nightgown, panties and with a coat wrapped around me. When we get to the hospital, the emergency room lobby is filled with people. One man holds his left arm while he stares into space. I'm guessing it's broken and he's waiting to get it put in a cask. There's another lady holding a screaming baby and a few other people who look sick but not deathly ill. Then there's one more woman sitting in the far corner of the lobby. She's sitting with her face in her hands and her back facing the crowd. The thing I notice most about this lady is that she's crying hysterically but nobody cares. There has to be at least 20 people in here and nobody's even paying her any attention. For some reason she reminds me of myself.

By the time we get to the counter I've calmed down quite a bit but I'm still crying. The lady at the desk told Chris that there might be a wait of about two hours because they're backed up. He tells her no and as I cry out again in pain she knows I have to be seen before many of the others. Chris fills out some paperwork and we wait about 30 minutes before they let me into the back of the emergency room to be seen by a doctor. The only person that went before me was the lady with the crying child. Right after she was called, a white lady said my name. We left the woman who was crying in the corner earlier, by herself, still crying.

When the doctor walks in he looks at me and immediately sees the pain I'm in. He asks me where it hurts, how long I've had this pain, why I haven't come to deal with this before now, and a few other questions. I feel stupid when he asks me why I haven't been to see a doctor about this before. The truth is I've always hated doctors. I've only been once or twice in my whole life and under those circumstances I wish I didn't have to go then.

The curly haired man, who looks to be fairly young, grabs a pair of latex gloves and glides his hands under my gown. He tells me to lie down while he presses down on my stomach. As soon as he puts a tiny bit of pressure on my stomach tears flow down my face.

"So it hurts there. Well how about here?"

I shake my head yes while Chris holds my hand.

"Excuse me sir but I am going to have to ask you to leave."

"What, I'm not going anywhere."

"Please sir, I need to give Ms. Smith a thorough examination."

"Chris it's okay. I'll be fine. Let the man do his job."

"But I know how you feel about this."

"I know but this time I'll be okay."

He leans down and kisses my cracked lips.

"I love you."

"Love you too."

Chris walks out and the doctor has already gotten all of the necessary equipment to give me a much-needed pap smear. He makes me slide down to the edge of the table and put my feet in the stir-ups.

"So how long have you been having these pains again?"

"Since I was around 24 or 25 years old."

"This will feel a bit uncomfortable but try to relax. Now is there anything that happened to you for you to have pains like this?"

I can't talk cause at this time he's already cranked open that thing inside my vagina. It feels so uncomfortable.

"Just take a deep breath."

I do. I breathe slowly while he takes samples from my insides with a long q-tip like thing. Once he has his samples and takes the instrument from between my legs I'm able to talk but don't.

"Ms. Smith can you please tell me how this happened. Why are you having these pains?"

"Well doctor it's actually a long story."

"Well I don't have all day but I still have to do a little more examining so why don't you go ahead and tell me."

"I don't know how to say this cause no one else knows about this. Only me and two other people and that's how I planned for it to stay. I never thought it would be a big deal until maybe a few months after it happened."

He holds up his left hand to tell me to hush for a moment while he inserts two fingers from his right hand back inside me. Then he presses down on my stomach wherever his fingers are. I almost cry when he does that.

"It hurts that bad huh."

"Yeah," I say crying much worse than before.

"I'm sorry mam, but I've got to see if what I suspect is true. So please finish your story, I won't interrupt anymore."

"Well, to make a long story short, I had an abortion. And no it wasn't by a real doctor like you but it was someone that I knew. I mean someone referred me to her and I went. I was young and didn't know what else to do. I'm so sorry."

The doctor watches me cry. I lay and cry some more while the doctor stands up and pats my legs as if to tell me I can move them now.

"I'm sorry too. I really don't even have to run any more test to know what's going to have to be done."

He tells me to sit up and put back on my panties.

"Do you want your husband to come in while I take this to our in-house lab and see what these samples show me?"

"No don't. Just tell me the truth. I'll be fine."

"Okay."

He pulls his stool close to me and looks me in the eyes.

"How old are you?"

"I'm 29."

"Do you have any children?"

"No, not yet."

"Well Ms. Smith I know this may be difficult for you to hear but I don't think you'll ever be able to have children."

I don't even blink. I lay back and let him finish.

"I can only imagine who and what kind of procedure was used to give you this abortion but it really did tear up your ovaries and uterus. I can't understand why you're just now getting in here with all of the pain you've been having. I'm sorry to tell you this but I'm gonna have to schedule you in here for a hysterectomy as soon as possible."

Again I feel my face getting wet, almost as if water is being pouring on me. My breath becomes slower but faster at the same time. I know I don't have asthma but I feel like I'm about to have an asthma attack. The doctor looks at me again. He doesn't seem startled and scared that I'm having an attack. He seems calm. I'm sure he sees this all the time. The way people seem like their gonna pass out or stop breathing but don't cause it's the initial shock of it all. Maybe it's the look that he gets from people when he tells them that their loved one has passed away or that a mother's child isn't gonna recover, or that somebody has a disease that's not curable. And I'm sure he gives them that same look. That look that says I'm sorry but there's nothing I can do. Like how he's giving me. The look of remorse, like he wishes he could make the pain go away and make me have more sense than to let some lady claiming to be mid-wife stick a rusty knife or whatever it was up in me to abort a child that I now wish I would have had.

"I'm so sorry. I'll leave you for a while but I'll be back to check on you."

With that he gets up rubs my hand in a comforting sort of way and leaves out of the room.

"Hey baby."

"Hey."

"The doctor told me it was okay to come in. Are you okay?"

"Yeah, I'm fine."

"Well what happened in here? What did the doctor say?"

"I really don't feel like talking about it right now."

"Listen I don't want you to feel like I'm pressuring you but I am going to be in your future. I'm here for you no matter what."

"Just hold me."

Chris rocks me like a father would his daughter and I cry silently in his arms.

"Chris I did some things in my life that I regret. I mean I regretted it the day I did it but after tonight I regret it even more. I really don't know how to tell you this but when I was young and in college I was dating this guy. He was in love with me. Maybe too much. Anyway, I thought he was supposed to be my husband. He was my first and back then I thought he was all there was. We went through two years of my college career in a relationship. Well, our breakup was nasty. A lot of cursing and fussing and screaming. And it wasn't his fault. I'm the reason he couldn't look at me the same. I was inexperienced and scared when it came to love and knowing what I know now, I would have done things differently."

"You were young, no one can blame you for what happened back then."

"I can. Cause everything that's happening to me now is directly related to what happened then. I really don't know how to say this to you cause I feel like I've finally got some order to my life. Just when I finally believe things can't get no worse this happens. Just when I think God's done punishing me, He's goes and does this. Goes and takes away the one thing I thought I'd always have. The one thing that makes me a woman."

"Ruthie what are you talking about?"

"I'm talking about why I been up screaming in pain these past years. I can't have children Chris. I can't have children."

"What? How does he know? We can go to another doctor and see what he says."

"No Chris, I can't have children. There's no need to consult with another doctor or a specialist or anything. I have to have a hysterectomy as soon as possible. Do you hear me? A hysterectomy."

Chris doesn't say anything. He looks at me and shakes his head. But I'm the one whose dreams have been crushed. Yeah he wanted kids but not with the same passion as me. Most women are brought up to raise a child. And I always wanted to have my own child to love and care for. He'll never understand why sex won't be the same. Why me watching parents walk with their kids will make me cry. I, like so many other women was born to raise a family and anything else seems foreign. Everything else seems foreign.

"I'm sorry. I'm so sorry. What do you want me to do?"

"There's nothing you can do."

"Well when is the operation?"

"Sometime soon. Whenever I set up a time with the doctor."

"Well, I'll just take off work so I can be here with you."

"No you don't have to do that."

"I'm about to be your husband and I'm going to be here for you. That's final."

I start to say no but don't. I just lay in the hospital bed wondering about the lady who was crying earlier in the waiting room. I wonder if her life has fallen apart like mine just has. I wonder what news the doctor could have given her to make her cry and wail and moan as she did. I wonder why she doesn't have any family to comfort her. I quickly stop thinking about her when the doctor knocks on the door. Chris says come in and the doctor immediately starts explaining a few details about the surgery and what it means for my future and so on. I don't really pay him any attention. My mind wonders back to the night I had the abortion done in the first place. I go over in my head the reasons and justifications I had for having it done. I even think of how Henry begged me not too. He practically pleaded with me to save his child and he would raise him. But I was young and dumb with no real faith in any man. I wish now I had listened to him cause now my dreams are over. While I drift in and out of consciousness, the doctor leaves and so does Chris. At this moment I feel like that lady must have felt as she sat out in the lobby crying while no one heard or understood why she cried in her own little space. I feel just like she looked. Alone and scared.

John

I'M LAYING IN the bed in some underwear and a t-shirt and Edna's laying beside me wit her head resting on my chest. I feel so uncomfortable. I'm comfortable but I'm uncomfortable at the same time. I feel kinda guilty bout laying here in the same bed me and Annabelle laid in for all those years. This the first time since Annabelle died that I been in here wit another woman. I done had some others but Edna the first that I thought enough of to bring back here. Not to mention the fact she made such a big deal bout it in the first place. And since I really like this one, ain't no need to mess it up now. Especially since we done had that talk and I done put all my dirty laundry out there for her to smell. She know everything that I been shame to tell anybody else. Even Annabelle. And it feels good to have lifted my burdens and have someone understand where I'm coming from and not shun me for doing some bad things in my day. I guess I could say I didn't know no better back then, but that ain't true. I was just selfish and stubborn. At least now I ain't as selfish as I used to be.

I wonder what Annabelle think bout some other woman lying in her bed. She probably turning over in her grave. I hope not but I might be turning over in mine if she was laid up wit some other man besides me. Here I am being selfish all over again.

"What you laughing at?"

I thought she was sleep.

"Nothing. Just thinking out loud."

"Well what you thinking bout."

"Nothing in particular just things. I told myself a joke and it was funny but nothing that would interest you."

"Oh."

"You alright."

"Yeah, I'm fine."

"Good. I want you to be."

We continue to lay in silence while Edna wraps her arms around me. I must doze off cause next thing I know, Edna's trying to wake me up.

"John get up, your daughter's on the phone."

"Huh, what you talking bout the phone didn't ring."

"Yes it did. Now here."

"Hello."

"Hey daddy."

"Sheila that you."

"Yeah it's me daddy."

I sit up in the bed.

"What's wrong?"

"No daddy, I just need you to come pick me up for work in the morning if you don't mind."

"No baby, I don't mind. But why you need me? Did James do something to you?"

"No daddy it ain't like that at all but I put him out Friday and he ain't been back and I need to get to work in the morning."

"Sheila, how long y'all gonna keep going on like this? You shouldn't let him treat you like this."

"Daddy I know."

"Did he hit you?"

"No daddy, you know he wouldn't ever hit me."

"You know what? I'm sick of him. Sick and tired of him treating you like you ain't shit."

"Daddy please don't be mad, everything's just fine. Trust me. I just needed some time to myself. Some time to sort my feelings out bout some things but me and James are just fine."

"Well if you say so. I'm not gonna fuss wit you bout it tonight."

"Good cause I don't feel like it. So daddy who answered the phone?"

I look over at Edna as she's staring me in my mouth.

"Well baby that's my lady friend Ms. Edna."

"Since when you got a lady friend?"

"Sheila can we talk bout that later."

"That's fine, I'm just wondering why I ain't met her yet."

"That'll come in due time. Okay."

"Alright daddy. Well I guess I'll see you in the morning."

"Okay."

"Don't forget, be here at around 6:15."

"I won't. I'll be up."

"Love you daddy."

"Love you too."

I turn over after hanging up the phone and lay with my back facing Edna. Women don't like that and she ain't no exception cause time I did it she huffing and puffing like I done did something wrong.

"Well what's wrong now?"

"Nothing."

"Now if you ain't gonna tell me now then don't come to me tomorrow talking bout what I already asked you."

"Why can't you just share with me what's going on with your family? I want to be involved too."

"Now Edna you here ain't you? You done answered my phone. Talked to my daughter. You laying in the bed wit me so what more do you want from me? You want me to tell you everything that happen as soon as it happens. Well I can't be like that. I'm not like that. Now you gone have to except me the way I am or else."

Edna don't say nothing cause I done hurt her feelings. She gets up and runs to the bathroom. Damn. She so sensitive. If I ain't telling her my life story then she ain't satisfied. I don't feel like trying to figure out what to do to make her feel like she wanted. I get out of bed, put on clothes, and head for the door. I'm not mad at her but I need to get out of this house. When I get outside and in the truck, Edna's at the door looking out the screen. I act like I don't see her and quickly drive off.

James

DAMN MAE. Why the fuck did she go to Sheila's job and tell her that. I shoulda went over there and slapped the hell out of her. Now Sheila done put me out the house and ain't no way I'm a keep staying at the shop. I done been laying on these chairs for two nights in a row but tonight my back hurt and I'm tired. I'm trying to do the right thing. I don't want no baby by some other woman and I know I ain't bout to claim no other child but for her to tell Sheila me and her still sleeping together is damn spiteful. Besides it just don't make no sense cause she didn't tell Sheila bout the baby. I don't know what's up wit Mae. She gone run all the way to Sheila's job just to say we still sleeping together but she ain't gone go head and tell her the whole thing. Sheila didn't notice her stomach? I guess not. I had to look hard at her to see it after she told me cause she wear all them big ass clothes. I guess she gone make it my responsibility to tell Sheila the rest. But I don't know if the baby mine. Hell Mae ain't no saint. It ain't like she might not have been messing wit somebody else. How I know for sure the baby mine? Even when I do try to tell Sheila she ain't gone listen. She so quick to blame me and she won't even listen to what I got to say. She wouldn't even let me tell her that I ended it wit Mae. That yeah it happened but not no more. What the fuck I'm gone do now? If Sheila find out bout the baby that's it. I know this is temporary but this the first time I'm a little scared that she won't forgive me. I wouldn't blame her if she didn't but this time I'm serious bout being there for her.

I ought to just go home. I already been gone two days. But I can't. I don't feel like fussing. I'm so sick of fussing. If it ain't one thing then it's another. One minute we on good terms, the next something like this come and fuck it up.

I been sitting out here in the parking lot for bout an hour now. Looking at the shop and contemplating whether I'm gonna go in or not. Hell I done drove round this town half the day and now I want to lay in my own bed. I want to cuddle up next to my wife. Besides who wants to be laying in some muggy ol shop. Maybe I'll go ask Charlie if he don't mind me sleeping on his couch tonight. Shit I done let him sleep on mine when Shirley had put him out for whatever reason. But he ain't no cheater and he treats Shirley good. Charlie loves that woman to death and she still treat him like shit. Either way it goes somebody's shitted on. Catch 22, I guess.

I get out the car. No need to get Charlie involved. Before I get out the car I open the glove compartment, reach in and get the plastic bag and my spare pint sized bottle of E & J. I slowly walk to the door and open it. I flip the switch to turn on the lights and then walk over to the 13" black and white TV. I don't cut it on cause TV goes off at around 11 and it's already a little after 10. I go over to my record player, gently lift the needle and put it on the record. After about five seconds of static, Marvin Gaye's, "Mercy, Mercy Me," comes on. Damn I love this song. It has to be one of my favorites of all time. When I first went to Vietnam in 72' it's the song that made me cry.

I sit down in one of the barber chairs and hold up my liquor. Nothing like a nice pint of something to make all of my troubles and worries go away. I twist off the cap and put the glass to my lips. With one gulp, ¾'s of the bottle is gone. It burns but not enough for me to put it down. It's the only thing besides women that I use to make me feel better.

I lift the bottle again but this time I only sip. I do this for about five minutes and then remember that I have something else that will definitely take my mind off things. I reach in my pocket and pull out the plastic bag. I get up, drop the bag in the chair and run to the closet. After I smoked in the hole the first time, I made my own pipe. Even though I haven't smoked no more since that one time, I knew it would come to this point. To the point where I wanted it bad enough. Or if something bad happened in my life, I knew I'd do it again. Funny thing is I don't even think it had to be something bad. Just a little something to make me go over the edge. Anything. Anything that make me nervous enough for the thoughts of Vietnam or the thoughts of my child dying come back.

After I get my homemade crack-pipe from underneath the cabinet behind the towels, I go back to my chair. I'm already tipsy from drinking all that liquor straight but I'm sober enough to remember how to do this. I grab the white rock from the bag and put it on top of the aluminum foil. Without any hesitation I put the flame to the bottle. I'm smoking. At first I cough a little, then I feel a little light-headed but after that I feel like a pro. Like I been doing this as long as some of them other people who hooked on it. I keep the flame going and keep smoking. When I'm done I feel like a bird. Almost as if I can fly away with one flap of the wings. Just as my eyes are closing and I'm ready to enjoy my high and listen to Marvin Gaye sing me to tears, the door opens.

I fumble with the bottle. It eventually falls to the floor. I turn around and look straight into the face of the man who's standing at the door.

"What you doing here?"

"No what you doing? I know you ain't on that stuff."

I stand up as the man comes towards me. Without any warning he punches me in the face. I fall on the floor and look up at him from a worm's eye view.

"Get up you little punk."

"Come on now don't hit me no more."

"You know what James, I'm sick and tired of you acting like a child rather than a man. You out here smoking on some dope and yo wife at home, calling me to come pick her up in the morning for work."

He kicks me in the stomach. I fall over in pain and stay there with my arms wrapped around my body. At first I don't recognize this man but I know his voice. I slowly turn around and lift myself up. I stand directly in front of him and notice that he's a little taller than me. My eyes meet his but I'm still slightly bent over.

"John please don't hit me no more. I'm sorry. It ain't really what you think. I ain't hooked on no drugs. You know how you try stuff. That's all. And besides Sheila put me out and that's the only reason I'm here in the first place."

"James I don't want to hear it. You a sorry ass man and if you don't straighten up I'm gonna really hurt you. That's my daughter you playing wit. That's my daughter who's trying to have your child again and you out here acting like a damn fool. Now why the hell she put you out anyway?"

"It's just a little misunderstanding."

"Tell me the truth."

"Well, this woman went to the job and—"

"What, you sleeping wit somebody else too?"

"Not no more. Wait John. Listen let me explain."

John walks over to the same chair I was sitting in, knocks the plastic bag on the floor and sits down. "I'm listening."

"Well before all this stuff happened wit me and Sheila, you know losing the baby and stuff, I was fine. The thoughts of Vietnam didn't bother me much and we were happy but after everything happened I just started doing stuff to get my mind off things. And that's where this lady Mae comes in. We messed around and now she saying that she pregnant wit my child. Sheila don't know all that but Mae went to her job. She went to her and told her that me and her was still, you know. Anyway that ain't true. I went and broke it off with her and I ain't been wit her since Sheila been back. I promise I been doing good. I haven't been out lately and I haven't been thinking bout drinking or no other women. It was just fine till that bitch went and told Sheila. Then she only told her that me and her was messing round not that she was pregnant. That's why I'm sitting here worried. I don't be getting high. Please John you got to understand."

He just looks at me and shakes his head. I'm still standing, just a little straighter now but I continue holding my stomach.

"James I understand but I still don't have no sympathy for you. You know better. And I don't care what kind of mistakes I done made in my life I ain't never once cheat on my wife. I loved her too much. But you, you don't have no respect or love for my daughter and that pisses me off. I can't stand her calling me in the middle of the night talking bout she need a ride to work in the morning."

He stands up and looks around before walking and standing directly in my face.

"Now son, I ain't gone tell you this but one time. If you ever hurt my daughter in any kind of way, I'll kill you. I promise I'll kill you. Sheila mean more to me than my own life so if you ever do anything to her that I don't like I'm gonna be looking for you wit my gun in my hand. Now you gone get yourself straight. You gone throw this shit out, stop being a child and act like a man."

He slaps me in the back of the head.

"You gone do what you have to do to make this problem you got go away. If you had any sense you'd just go head and tell Sheila the truth bout this other baby that may or may not be yours. Then on top of all that you gonna go pick Sheila up for work in the morning. And next time you ought to, no better yet, you better leave the car to the house so she won't have to worry bout no ride. And James if you think I'm playing, try me. Do you understand me?"

I shake my head yes as he walks pass me, then out the door.

Ruthie

CHRIS AND I are lying in the bed and I'm tossing and turning. I have to be to the hospital in four days. I'm so scared. Not so much because I'm having the surgery but because of what will happen after it. I'm confused and scared and can't sleep so all I've been doing tonight is watching the clock, running to the bathroom and crying lightly on my pillow. I'm sure Chris is up cause he's not moving. That's how I know he's woke. He usually tosses and turns or at least kicks his leg several times a night but tonight nothing.

All I can think about is why me and what will we do now that we know I can't have children. Will Chris have second thoughts about marrying me because of this? Besides that, how will I feel? I've heard from a few people that when a woman has a hysterectomy they become closed from their family and friends and feel like less of a woman. I can understand why cause your uterus is a big part of being a woman. It allows you to reproduce and have children, which seems to be the primary reason women were created in the first place.

I don't know how to feel. I wanted children so bad at one point. So bad that it hurts me to even think about it. I guess that's why I keep crying. I've flipped my pillow at least three times in the last three hours cause I keep soaking each side. Damn I've got to pee again. I've been to the bathroom four times already and I know Chris is sick of me getting up. He already fusses at me for having to use the bathroom so much. He's always like, "not again, you just went to the bathroom." He sounds so cute when he says it in that annoyed voice. But he hasn't said anything to me tonight. Maybe he's too disappointed to talk to me. That's probably the thing that makes me cry the most. Thinking about losing the person who loves me the most. I've never known a man who cares so much. I'm so afraid he might not want me after this surgery. He's probably just sticking around to make sure I'm okay but afterwards I'm sure he'll leave me here all alone.

I can't hold it no more. I jump up and run down the hall, again. When I finish and get back to the room the light is still off but Chris is sitting up in bed.

"What's wrong Chris?"

"Nothing, but with you running to the bathroom every five minutes how can a man get some sleep round here. You know that's ridiculous that you've gone to the bathroom five times tonight. You need to get that checked out."

I giggle.

"Chris I can't help it. I've always had to go to the bathroom like this," I say as I get back in the bed.

"I'm just saying."

"Well."

We both lay back down. Our backs are facing each other as we both try desperately to get in a comfortable position. Chris sits back up.

"Ruthie are you okay?"

"Yeah, why do you ask me that?"

"Because you seem to be a little distant right now. I know everything that's going on has to be stressful but it seems like there's something else."

"What do you mean?"

"Well you won't talk to me anymore and take tonight for instance. You're tossing and turning and it's obvious you've been crying but you won't even tell me what's on you're mind. Talk to me."

"Chris are you going to be able to handle this?"

"Handle what?"

"This. Everything that's happening. Me not being able to have children. That means it's over for you too if you still plan on spending—"

"If. If what. Ruthie I'm not going anywhere."

"Listen, the fact is I can't have children no matter what. Don't you understand they're going to take the very thing that makes me a woman in a matter of days. I'm the one that wanted children."

"Hold on. Just stop. Listen you're not the only one who's affected by this or have you forgotten. Or better yet do you even care about how I feel. I want children but..."

"But what."

"But we can't have them and I've accepted it. Well I'm trying to accept it. I'm hurting too. I wanted children. I've always believed that I would have a family and raise a son and daughter so don't even sit here and act like I'm the selfish person that isn't feeling anything. Cause I am. I'm hurting too, just like you."

"I'm sorry Chris, I didn't realize—"

"I know cause you didn't ask. You never ask. The fact is, I don't know how I feel about not being able to have children. Yeah I've accepted it but at the same time I haven't. I haven't been able to sleep all night thinking about the fact that soon it's gonna be over. I know you're the woman I want to spend my life with and I love you with all my heart but am I willing to sacrifice not having any kids? That's what I'm struggling with. I'm sorry but that's the way I feel."

"Chris I understand exactly what you're saying. I can understand it if you need your time to sort things out. To see if you can live without children because of some stupid mistake I made years ago that had nothing to do with you."

"Ruthie I'm not saying I don't love you but you're right, I do need time. Time to clear my head. Everything's happening so fast. It seems like just the other day I was asking you to marry me and now we find out this."

"Well don't worry about me. I'll be fine. You might as well go now. Go sort your feelings and get your head cleared. I need to be by myself anyway."

"But I want to be there with you while you're in the hospital."

"Trust me, I'll be fine. It'll only take a couple of hours and when I'm well rested and back home I'll call you so we can talk. Please don't argue, just go do what you have too. I don't need you to be with me when I get the procedure done. I'll be fine."

"But—"

"But nothing. Go on. I don't need you with me. Chris I love you. And I love you enough to let you go. So go ahead and figure out where you see us. Please, no arguing. Just go."

With that, Chris sighs heavily, grabs his shoes and coat, walks out of the bedroom, down the stairs, and out my life.

John

"**ALRIGHT JOHN I** over reacted. So I want to apologize right now before we even go any further."

"Well, I just walked in the house so if I can just take off my shoes and get out these clothes I'd feel a whole lot better."

"Okay. I'll wait till you take your bath and stuff."

I slowly walk past Edna and head straight for the bathroom. I turn on the hot water, put my hand underneath it, then add a little bit of cold. I don't put in the stopper; instead I pull the knob and let the water come flowing down. I take off my clothes and step into the hot shower. I stand directly underneath the water and let it beat on my body. This water feels so good. I stand and feel the heat sooth me. I keep my eyes open while the water washes my face. As I continue to stand not washing at all, I feel a little lightheaded. First, I put my hand on the wall to keep my balance, then I grab the soap. I try to wash through the dizziness cause I really don't feel like sitting down. I keep rubbing the soap on my body until I think I'm clean enough. After turning off the water I step out the tub and place my long bare feet on the floor. I stare at my feet for a minute as they press deep into the blue rug. I take a towel from the cabinet and slowly put the lid down on the toilet so I can sit down.

While I was walking last night my breath kept getting short. And it wasn't cause of the age. It felt different like I was bought to pass out. I kinda had a little bit of tightness in my chest too. It didn't matter cause I just kept right on walking. It feels like I been walking all night. I practically have cause my truck broke down soon as I left James's shop. I was on my way back home and then the truck go making some kind of noise. Next thing I know, I was pulling over to side of the road. I figured it was the alternator. I knew it was bout to give but I thought it would keep me on the road a little longer. I tried to do a quick fix and play wit the starter and engine but that didn't work so I ended up walking. Nowhere in particular, just walking. I walked until daybreak and now here I am, back home. I guess I needed to walk cause I feel pretty good now. Now I can go in here and listen to whatever Edna got to say and apologize for walking out on her like that. I wish I could give her what she wants. I can but she got to be patient and me telling her that ain't doing no good. So she gone have to figure that out herself.

Right now I can't even think bout her. I'm more concerned wit Sheila and this situation James done got himself in. I can't even look at James without trying to kill him. He makes me sick but my baby want him and the bad thang is ain't nothing I can do bout it. Last night he made me so mad. And then him in that shop smoking that dope. On top of that he supposed to have some other woman pregnant wit his child. That gone kill Sheila.

But as crazy as it seems, as much as I hate James I envy him at the same time. He a whole lot more of a man than I ever was as far as being the man of his house. He got total control. Cause when Sheila tell James to get out, it ain't for good it's just to scare him a little but he knows that that's why it don't never work. I almost walked out on Annabelle a couple of times but she was so strong, she'd say "gone get outta here if you want to." Hell that alone made me not want to leave. I needed her to need me but whenever she let me know she didn't, I just went back to her. Cause fact of the matter was, she didn't need me, I needed her. I member one day I tried to break bad and hit Annabelle. I had just worked my fifth 12-hour day straight and when I walked in the house she was in the back with Ruthie. Ruthie musta been bout five or six months and me and Annabelle was having a hard time getting along wit each other. Every time I looked at Ruthie I felt like a complete failure and Annabelle couldn't understand why. Hell at first I didn't even hold Ruthie or go see bout her when she cried at night. By the seventh month I was just starting to act like I was her father in some ways. I would give her a bottle every now and then or change her if Annabelle was busy.

But it was on that night after working all day when I was tired and irritated, that I came home and crossed the line. It seemed like the slightest thing woulda set me off and on that night my food wasn't nowhere in sight. Well Annabelle musta heard me come in and shut the door cause she hurried and came running down the hall. She was so happy. Her face was bright and her eyes was gleaming like she was on top of the world.

"Hey John, I was just putting Ruthie down but yo food—"

Slap.

I didn't even let her finish her sentence fore I had slapped her cross the face. When I did it I felt kinda bad but I wouldn't let her see that. I had never slapped a woman before cause my daddy did it so much to my momma I vowed not to do it to my own wife but on that day all of my promises and values disappeared. So we stood there. Me looking at her and Annabelle just sorta standing wit her head turned away from me.

She didn't move, she just took her left forefinger and wiped the blood away from the corner of her mouth. She stayed still for a long time as if she was thinking bout hitting me back. She didn't. She just lifted her head and looked me straight in the eyes. And me thinking I'm tough stood there in sort of a daring way. I was practically begging her to do something back. So we continued to stand there, she staring at me like a hawk and me shying away cause her eyes made me uneasy. It's amazing how her confidence made a 6-foot-4 grown man back down from an almost 6-foot woman. I continued to stand but my shoulders began to slouch and head began to bow, while her back held no curve and her eyes never blinked. I waited for her reaction. To my surprise the next words out of her mouth were "in the oven." Then she walked to the kitchen and put my plate on the table. I thought I had won. I sat down, ate and was served but the moment I was done and my fork hit the plate, Annabelle had a knife to my neck. I always wondered how she got to me so quick without me seeing it coming first.

"If you ever hit me or think bout hitting me again I'll kill you. I'll kill you just as sho' as I'm standing here."

I didn't move or speak. Hell I couldn't cause she had the blade pressed up against my Adam's apple and to tell you the truth I was scared. Shit, no man had ever put fear in me like she did at that moment. And I mean I never walked around fearing my woman but I knew I couldn't and would never treat her like my dad did my mom. She demanded respect and from that moment on, I never disrespected her in that way again. My momma always told me that if you push the right woman the wrong way, she'll hurt you. Too bad she wasn't the right woman or she woulda killed my daddy long time ago.

Meanwhile I was sitting there wit sweat bedding up on my forehead and underneath my arms. After bout five minutes of her holding the knife wit a steady hand and heavy breathing, she let it fall into my lap. That almost made me pee in pants. The thought crossed my mind to grab the knife but I knew a gun would be to my temple next, so I pushed it on the floor and spent the night on the couch. As a matter of fact I spent several hungry nights on that couch until I got up enough courage and sense to apologize.

After that Annabelle always left my plate sitting on top of the stove if they had already eaten. I guess that was more to avoid her killing me as opposed to me hurting her. But it was hard feeling like less of a man in yo own house. Feeling like you ain't running nothing. Yeah, I brought home the food and the clothes, but once I stepped foot in that house, Annabelle took over. I still disciplined the children but Annabelle ruled me. She had food on the table when I walked in the door but if I thought she was going to serve me or always sit there with me while I was eating, I was wrong. It was whatever she wanted. If she didn't feel like being bothered, you can best believe she wouldn't. But she was still the type who was struggling with something. I never understood why, she seemed strong but weak at the same time. In the end that's the same thing that killed her.

I guess James situation a little different from mine but he still got skeleton's in his closet and secrets that need to be revealed. Just like me. The difference with him is that he done lost two kids and done fought in a war that wasn't his to be bothered wit in the first place. And now his scars finally coming out. I can see it in his eyes. He hurt and can't handle it. So he done turned to smoking dope and sleeping wit every other woman in town. Being hurt done drove me to do things I'll always regret and I hope James don't make the same mistakes I did.

I reckon Edna think I'm trying to avoid her cause I been sitting on this toilet for bout a half hour just thinking. I get on up, wrap the towel around my body and open the bathroom door. I walk straight to my room and pull out some white underwear and a pair of old pants. I slip them on and then go into the living room where Edna is sitting patiently waiting.

"John, you feel better."

"Yeah I do, but listen. Before you say anything, I'm sorry."

"Me too."

"Lets not even talk about it okay. We gone be okay."

Edna gets up off the sofa and walks over to me. We hug for a while and then I cook breakfast.

Shelia

The other morning James came to pick me up. When I heard the car pull up I thought it was my dad and so I didn't look outside. I kept getting dressed. Then the front door just came open. I mean I heard the key in the lock but I didn't pay it no attention cause daddy got a key too. Well it wasn't daddy and I was real surprised. I never would have thought that James would have thought enough of me to come pick me up for work even though we having problems. He told me he figured I told my dad. He said he caught him just in time. Anyway we didn't say much to each other at first. I mean he said morning and I said the same thing but nothing much after that. At around 6:20 I told him I was ready to go. We left and guess what, he opened the door for me. Do you know how many years it's been since he's opened the door for me? Probably since we first starting courting. Well once we were both in the car, we sat in silence till we got to my job. Right when I was bout to get out the car he grabbed my hand and told me how much he loved me and how sorry he was that Mae

came to my job and said those things. He also said that he had
something he needed to talk to me about and that we would get things
right. He even told me that even though he had been with Mae in the
past he wasn't no more. He promised. I can't say that he lying cause
he usually don't promise me stuff. He usually don't just out right lie.
Well I hope he telling me the truth cause James don't know how I felt
when that woman came to my job. That really is something that you
get your ass kicked over. If I wasn't pregnant I woulda hit her in the
face. I'm much bigger so I know I coulda beat her up easy. I ain't
lost too many fights in my day and even if I did, the woman had a hell
of a fight on her hands. She just got on my nerves so bad. It was
humilliateing sitting there listening to some woman tell you that she
sleeping wit your husband. It just made me feel like I was worthless.
Besides that she come in the schoolhouse and marched to the
cafeteria. That's my job. Don't come on no woman job and expect
them to act like somebody when you come wit some bullshit. I coulda
respected her more if she came to my house like a woman and even
then you still get your ass kicked. So I guess it's good I'm pregnant
cause she woulda been one hurt sista. She came this close. I swear
she did. Even though she look a lot bigger since last time I seen her
wit that big ol house dress on, I'm still sure I could beat her ass. Only
if I wasn't pregnant and even then, I started to slap the taste out her

mouth. But she come telling me how James been out to her house all these nights but none of them any time recently. It's been months ago except for the other night. Well I don't say nothing, I just listen and shake my head. Just shake my head cause all the time I'm thinking James doing good. But the one thing that got me is that she said she had more to tell me. She even got a little look in her face that let me know she wasn't playing no games wit me and that she needed to say something else. She got real woman like and asked me could she come over to the house one day but not till the time was right. I told her no at first but then I said just come on over and make what you got to say quick. She even ended up apologizing for coming to my job cause she ain't mean no harm but she couldn't take it no more. She said that after she got this last thing off her chest she ain't gone bother me no more. Hell we ain't never gone be friends but I figure that since she came back a little better I might as well listen to what she got to say. So she posed to come over one day. I don't think it gone be no time soon cause she said when the time was right. I wonder what she mean by that. We ain't gone sit around wit no dinner or nothing and I even told her that she had to tell me from the porch and that I would have a knife in my hand if she wanted to act crazy. I just don't know what to think. James don't seem to be doing nothing that he don't got no business doing. He come home after work, he don't be out late so I don't want to believe it. I mean I don't think he would still be cheating but then how do I know. I want to trust him but sometimes I just can't. I did think that him coming to get me the other morning said a lot. I felt good about that. He called my dad without me even knowing and told him not to get me. He came instead. I feel real good bout that. But at the same time I feel like, well I don't know. The doctor's told me that when I feel well, sort of depressed then I should write. I did decide to wait till I got home. I just needed to make sure I was alone. James don't even know that I do this writing. He got no clue that when I feel bad and down that I don't try to talk to him no more, I just talk to this here book. If he ever knew that, he'd probably have a fit. But sometimes I don't know what James be thinking. He know Mae don't care for me so why he go be with someone that don't like me. Its plain disrespectful if you ask me. You can't just go around sleeping wit people and especially those that don't like your wife. James know better and I feel so.... I don't know. I'm so unsure about what steps to take. If I had the strength or the courage to get up and leave, I might be better off. Maybe before this baby but now I just can't. It's almost like I depend on James for life itself rather than depending on myself. My momma was never like that. She loved my daddy but somehow it seemed like his love was just a little stronger for her. Instead of it being the other way round, like it's posed to. My momma did do his fingernails, though. I always loved it when she did his nails, it always seemed like they were so happy. Momma always took her time too. She used to get the file and a pail with warm water and soap and lotion. Me and Ruthie would sit around and talk about our day and momma and daddy would make us laugh. That's probably the only time we was truly happy. Ruthie and my daddy seemed to get along good too. They didn't argue and he didn't criticize her. We all just sat down and talked. Everyone of us looked forward to those treats once a month or if we were lucky two times a month until they stopped all together. I always wondered why momma quit doing his nails all of a sudden. It just seems like my momma was so strong and fearless and never made no mistakes. And I know she woulda left my daddy if he treated her half as bad as James has been treating me. My daddy wasn't no saint but he was nothing like James. I'm sure the only bad thing my daddy ever did was beat Ruthie real bad. I didn't even tell nobody bout that. I'm the only one who knew what happened but I think it woulda hurt momma too bad. And every since the night that he told me to trust him and not say nothing, I did it. I did it without even questioning him or asking him if it was wrong. I didn't want him to be at odds wit momma. Sometimes I feel like I shoulda told somebody what happened but I can't. I trust him too much. He told me that everything was fine and I didn't have no reason to doubt him. He my daddy. I guess that's why I trust James so much. I know I shouldn't just because he's broken that trust so much but I just do cause I gotta. He's all I got and I ain't known nothing but to trust my dad even when he was wrong so I guess I oughta trust James too.

Ruthie

"BUT DADDY."

"But nothing. Come here."

"But daddy."

He grabbed my hand and snatched me over closer to him. He quickly pulled off his belt and lifted it in the air. I looked closely in his eyes and noticed the rage and guilt that had taken over his pupils. He continued to hold the belt in the air before finally bringing it down and pounding on my butt.

"Now how many times have I told you to take yo ass to sleep when you go to bed?"

I stood without an answer. Tears came strolling down my cheeks, which only enraged him more.

"Huh? Didn't you hear me ask you a question," he said as he smacked me again with the belt.

I still didn't answer and he continued to hit me while saying "huh, didn't you hear me."

I started crying uncontrollably while trying to break loose. He tightened his grip while my head and body twisted and turned. I looked and saw Sheila peeping around from the room, watching and crying along with me.

I jump up and blink but I can't see. Complete darkness surrounds me. My eyes won't come open. It's like they're sealed shut. I lay back down and start crying. I'm not sure why the tears seep through my closed eyes but they do. Maybe because the dream came back. Again another scene revealed. Another piece to a night that I can't remember. I let the tears fall onto my cheeks then down onto my neck making it feel sticky and soggy like when I was a child. I don't move for a while. I lay for a while longer without any movement. I don't hear much but there are sounds. First there's a flash of beeps that continue in maybe two-second intervals. Besides that, I hear a constant buzz coming from the right of me. Now I hear snoring. Someone's in here with me. I listen to everything that's going on around me but it's still minimal compared to the noise in my mind. The dream. My dad. The spanking. His eyes. Sheila's watching. Her crying. My crying. What went on that night? I've got to know. Why was my dad so mean? Why did his face show so much indifference? Maybe it's because I'm not his. Maybe he just hated me.

I move my head from side to side and then try to blink a few times. Finally my eyes begin to creep open. I rub the wetness from them and see light appear where there wasn't any. I can see. I'm in a hospital room. My pupils dart from one side of the room to the other. I see the beeping noise. It's the monitor. I turn to my left and there's a curtain. It's separating me from the snores. My expression changes from total sadness to somewhat relief. I'm still out of it but at least my eyes will open. I turn my head again and lift my right hand but it hurts. An IV. It hurts. I slowly put my arm back down before I hear and watch the door open.

"Ms. Smith, I see you're up now."

"Yes," I mumble.

"So how do you feel?"

"I'm okay, I guess."

"Well everything is done and you're gonna be fine. You shouldn't have any more problems. We did—"

"What, it's done?"

"Yes mam. You came in at about 6:30 and we got started an hour later and now it's 12 o'clock. We've been finished for a little while now and I guess the anesthesia is just now wearing off."

"Oh."

"Well, if you need anything just push that button beside you. It's connected directly to the nurse's station. I'll be back shortly to check on you. Get some rest okay."

I don't respond. I simply watch the young doctor walk out the room as I lay lonely with an aching wrist. I couldn't find the words or sound needed to tell him the IV hurts. All I could think about was the fact that it was done. All the years of the uncertain periods and the cramping and the aches and the headaches and the guilt and the sporadic pain during sex and the abortion and the metal utensils, the hanger, the knife, the blood, the emptiness. All of it's gone. But not only is the pain gone but also the hopes and dreams.

Before it was just knowing that this day would come but now that it's a reality, it feels different. The pain's just a little deeper and a little stronger. Right now I'd rather have the physical pain cause I'm sure it wouldn't hurt as bad as this. Cause with this it doesn't matter how many pain killers you take, no matter how many doctor visit's you make the hurt will remain. Right now I feel numb. I can't cry but there are tears. Somewhere. There are cries that haven't been released yet. There are moans that I can't seem to let out. I've cried so much before the procedure was done. I cried simply at the thought but in reality this is much worse.

Someone knocks on the door. I don't say anything because I don't feel like being bothered. The door squeaks open anyway. I don't look towards the entrance, I close my eyes. I'm tired. Whoever it is doesn't speak and I don't let them know I'm up. I stay still and listen to the person pace the room and then stand by the door. I keep waiting, hoping they will leave. They don't, instead I feel someone sit in the chair next to my bed. The scent is familiar. I quickly turn my head to my left and open my eyes.

"What are you doing here?"

"I was in the neighborhood so I went by your apartment. Your fiancé was there. He told me you were here."

"Who, Chris?"

"Unless you've got more than one."

"No that's him, I'm just trying to figure why he's there."

"Well, I'm trying to figure why he's not here."

"It's a long story. The better question is what are you doing here?"

"Ruthie, no matter what happened between us, I still consider you my friend. My best friend."

"Well, I'm not so sure about that. You forgot about being my friend long time ago. Remember."

"Listen, I didn't come to argue. I came because I know how difficult this must be for you. I just wanted to see how you were doing."

"Well you've seen so—"

"Don't do that Ruthie, please."

"Do what?"

"Be so fucking sarcastic and not caring."

"Why? I've been waiting a long time to say something to you. When you left me, I needed you. I was hurt. Not only physically but emotionally and you walked out the door. After all our plans you walked out on me. I was willing to be everything to you. To be what we were both ashamed of and scared to admit. I destroyed everything for you. Everything that I could have had is gone.

"You knew me better than anyone else and I loved you more than anyone else but you walked out on me to be with the family you claimed not to even love. So I'm sorry if I don't feel like celebrating because you're here. Don't you realize, I opened up with you like I've never done with anyone else in my life, in the most intimate ways and right now I can't even look at you."

"I'm sorry."

"Sorry for what."

"For hurting you. I loved you too. In fact—"

"Listen don't be sorry. I'm fine. Yeah, I've had a hard time getting over you. But the real problem has been finding a person to trust the way I trusted you."

"And have you found that?"

"Maybe."

"Well, I didn't come to upset you. I really have missed you and I wanted us to get back to where we were."

"Really."

"For real. I'm ready now."

"How's Bill? Don't even say it Carmen. I think it's time for you to leave."

There is a brief pause and then another knock.

"Come in."

"Baby, you're up. I came by earlier but you were sleep."

"You've been here," I say trying to focus my attention away from Carmen.

"Yeah, but I didn't come in cause I wanted to talk to you when you were up and feeling better."

"Well let me go."

"Ahh, this is Carmen," I say in an uneasy voice.

"Yeah, I met her earlier. You doing alright?"

"I'm okay. Just leaving though."

"Don't let me rush you off."

"You're not. It's time for me to leave."

Carmen stands up and turns towards me.

"I hope everything works out for you Ruthie." She leans down kisses me on the cheek and then whispers, "I still love you" in my ear. I don't move, just lie there frozen in that moment. I see her walk to the door but I'm stuck in another place. Almost taken back to when we were something more than just memories to each other. Once I hear the door close and Chris's dragging voice, I snap out of my trance.

James

WHEN I WALK into the house, Sheila's sitting at the kitchen table with her hands covering her face. Those hands seemed to have aged 10 years in only three cause her veins are now beginning to rise to the surface and wrinkles are forming on her caramel colored skin.

"What's wrong now? For the past three months we been fine so what could I have done now for you to be sitting here looking like that."

She don't say nothing. She just keeps on looking at the wedding picture that's hanging on the wall. I member that day. It was a hot day in June when me and Sheila got married at the Courthouse but had a big reception at *Lucky's*. Balloons and ribbons covered the place. The food was set up nicely and *Lucky's* was transformed into a classy reception hall. Everybody was waiting on us and we had so much fun. We both were so happy on that day. But tonight as Sheila continues to stare at the picture I realize we will never be back in that moment again. Never be as happy as we were on that day. Never as satisfied and never as content. Life has become hard. So have we.

"Sheila come on, tell me what's wrong?"

Without even looking up, she starts talking, "Yeah, Mae came over tonight."

"What? What she come over here for?"

"You know good and damn well why she came over. She came to tell me and show me everything that you wouldn't. Everything that you didn't love me enough to say. I gave you another chance and before you even got back in the door you had already broken my heart again."

"What you talking about? I ain't been messing wit her no mo."

Sheila puts her hands on the top of the table and pushes herself up onto her feet. Her face is now staring at mine but her stomach is the only thing that separates us.

"See I knew you would say something like that but it don't matter. I just need for you to leave. Just get out and don't come back. No more."

"Listen baby, we can make this right. Don't let that bitch come over here and ruin what we working hard for," I say as I kneel down on both knees at the same time.

As I look up in her face it reads disgust and anger. She looks like she's finally had enough of me. Enough of my jiving and messing around. Enough of my lying and cheating. She for real this time. If she ain't ever been serious before she serious now and I can tell cause I can see it in her face. The way she ain't even crying, she just looking sad and pitiful and hurt like she done cried enough and can't find tears to make em' come out.

"Man I can't believe you can sit here and act like everything's going to be alright. You must think I'm some kind of fool or something. I mean a woman comes over to my fucking house and says she's gone have yo baby and you think I'm supposed to just sit here and say nothing. And she bigger than me. So she gone have the baby that I may never have."

"You mean to tell me you gone believe the bullshit she got to say even though she been fucking every other man in the whole fucking town," I say standing back up on my feet.

"James you mean to tell me you want me to believe she lying when I looked in her eyes like I'm looking in yours."

"We don't know fo sure if the baby mine. I told her to get rid of it anyway, shit she don't know who the father is. She just mad cause I won't leave you for her."

We both standing eye level with each other, not blinking, just staring at each other. I'm trying not to be the first person to look down but I can't stand to see her like this. I know for sure there's nothing I can say or do cause she want me out.

"Baby I'm sorry, I'm so sorry. This is all my fault," I say finally looking away and pacing the floor. I suddenly start crying but it don't do nothing to Sheila. She just looks at me and kinda shake her head.

"None of this would be like this, you and me would still be happy. We would still be a family, if I would just stop being so fucking selfish and if I could just control...If we hadn't lost—"

"I don't want to hear that. We are going to have a family. We could still be a family. Don't you understand," Sheila says while walking over and softly wiping the tears from my cheeks.

"James, you can't use my miscarriage and stillborn as an excuse for you cheating on me and making me have to go through this alone. They was my children too and I just can't take no more. I'm almost due and we still going through this bullshit.

When will we get through this? When will you stop being high and drunk long enough to be here for me again? I need you so much but."

"You're right. It's my fault, I won't do nothing else like this. It's my fault that we going through this….all my fault. I'm the one who's been messing round not you. You don't deserve this and it'll stop. The moment Mae told me bout this pregnancy I almost went crazy. I left her alone that same night. I promise. I promise, please believe me that after I moved out that last time I wasn't messing wit her. And I wanted to tell you. I wanted to tell you that she was pregnant and she was blaming it on me but I couldn't. I couldn't find the words to break your heart. Besides the baby might not be mine. Please believe me. Baby please just give me one mo chance. I promise. For real, this is it. It's me and you from now on."

Sheila shifts her weight from her right to her left foot, leans back over slightly to the right and folds her arms across her chest.

"James I'm sorry. I just need some time to think. You got to leave."

Sheila walks pass me to the hallway, grabs a heavy black suitcase and brings it to the kitchen.

"These some of your things. I went on and packed em' cause I just need some time."

"What? You mean to tell me you done packed my shit and now you trying to put me out my own house. That worked last time but not now. I'm ain't going no fucking where."

"James don't do that, let's not go through this. It's just for a few weeks so I can get my mind straight. I just need to get through this pregnancy. Get through it this time.

Don't you want that? Just go on over to yo momma's house," Sheila says while handing

me the package full of clothes. I look down at the suitcase and then back up at Sheila.

Out of nowhere I knock the suitcase out of her hands. The suitcase somehow slides to the

bottom of the white stove. My mind goes back and forth from Vietnam to the present

until I hear Sheila's voice. She's moaning slightly while she grabs the inside of her hand

where the handle scraped her fingers.

"I ain't going no where. This my house."

I then bend down on the floor and unlatch the sliver buckles on the suitcase and

start throwing my clothes all over the floor.

"Stop James."

"No fuck that. If you think, I'm leaving my house again you wrong."

I keep throwing clothes on the floor. I mumble something under my breath but I

don't even know what I'm saying. Next thing I know, Sheila starts reaching for me. She

grabs my left arm wit both of her hands. When I turn to face her she must see something

cause she's scared. Maybe she sees the rage that I feel right now. So we just sort of stop

and look at each other and I realize she looks strange. Not like the Sheila I know.

Almost foreign. I keep looking at her. At her eyes and mouth and hair and I realize that

she's not Sheila. I snap. I push her on the floor and stand over her. Then I quickly grab

her by the neck but only to slap her back down again. Her eyes are now real big and her

lips are shaking. But it can't be her. She looks sort of like one of those Vietnamese

women that we went in and murdered for no reason cause they was in the way of some

kind of mission we were on. I close my eyes but when I open them back, she still looks

different so I slap her face again. She almost blocks the hit but her reflexes are too slow.

I watch the blood trickle down her lip and then without even thinking, I start choking her. I just shake her with my bear hands and grab as hard as possible. She's trying to fight back but I tell her to stop, don't make it so hard. I'm scared cause it's been so long since I been in this kind of war. And it was so much easier cause I knew who the enemy was. It was them. They were the ones who we were sent to kill. I keep looking at the woman whose eyes are rolling in the back of her head. She's starting to look familiar again. I squint my eyes to see if maybe I done made a mistake. It's Sheila. Sheila the one who look like she bout to die. I quickly take my hands from round her neck. Once I release my grip, I try to see if Sheila's alright.

"I'm so sorry baby, I didn't mean it. Now get up."

She don't say nothing, she just lay there on the floor staring into space. She suddenly opens her mouth but no sound comes out.

"Sheila baby say something."

She seems to be in shock. So much so that she starts reaching out for something. She reaches her arms out in the air and keeps them there for a while until she finally finds the strength to crawl away from me.

"What you doing Sheila? What's wrong? Who do you see? I'm sorry. I'm so sorry baby, please come back. I didn't know who you was."

Once she's closer to the doorway she grabs an arm full of air and holds on to it as if it's something important to her survival.

"Everything's okay baby, mommy's alright."

"What, who you talking too?"

I can't stand to see her like this and I can't believe what I've just done. I sit on the floor and start hitting myself in the head until I hear Sheila scream.

I walk into the hospital room with my head down. I'm still ashamed about what happened. I can't explain it. One minute I was fine the next minute I'm bout to kill the one woman I love more than myself. As I watch Sheila move into a more comfortable position, I look at her face. She's still asleep. Her lip is puffy and she looks weak. Her face appears to be worn. It's been such a long night. I can't believe it. Of all the women I've been with, I chose the only one I loved to hit. I mean after I hit Mae I didn't feel bad cause I almost felt like she deserved it but Sheila, not Sheila. She doesn't deserve to be put through any of this bullshit that she's been through. I almost killed her. I just can't bear the thought of her leaving me. Besides that I know she loves me. So much. She would die for me and I would do the same for her. And when she went outside of herself once again that's what almost killed me. The fact that she actually thought our child was standing there. She was talking to an image and it was because once again I had pushed her over the edge.

I can hardly remember everything. I know things got out of hand but I didn't realize how bad until she screamed. When she hollered, I snapped out of whatever it was I was going through and went to her rescue. The fact is, I been having these little lapses in my mind every since I got back to the states and now I know that I got to get em' under control. It takes something like this for me to realize that I'm the cause for everything. I knew it but I didn't truly believe it till now. I'm the reason she been writing in that book to control herself from going off the deep end again. Sheila don't know I know bout that book she keep hid underneath the mattress. After Mae told her bout the affair and I finally got back in the house, I came home early to surprise Sheila with dinner. She must have been startled so she left it out on the nightstand and while she was in the tub, I read some of what she had wrote. After I read the first couple of pages I couldn't read no more. I just couldn't listen to her talk about me like that and how she felt when she was having the breakdown. I knew she was hurting but not that much. I didn't realize she needed me so much. I knew I should have told her bout Mae accusing me of being the baby's daddy. If I would have just been a man about things, none of this would have happened.

Now it seems like I'm back in 1975. Back at the beginning of all of this. Me and Sheila done come full circle almost. Me walking back into the hospital room trying to find the words to say to Sheila once again. Us in the same place we were a couple years ago. The hospital. I feel like I done been down this road so many times before. So many times I done had to try to control my tears and hide my emotions just to get words to come out my mouth.

I know my eyes are red cause they burning. I been in this hospital for what seems like weeks. I ain't even had the nerve to call Sheila's daddy cause I know he gone try to kill me once he see Sheila and find out what I done. I've been doing so much thinking. My mind is finally clear. See when Sheila screamed it was so familiar. It sounded the same way it did the first time. Lord knows that's the thing that woke me up. That's the sound that snapped me out of my own thoughts. I knew right at that moment something was wrong. After we got to the hospital, they didn't let me in the room. They closed them two doors and that was it. It took a long time for the doors to open again.

Before I knew it, I was on my knees praying to God, crying once again for mercy. And now it's time to tell Sheila.

Since I walked into the room, I've come quite close to her. I'm practically standing over her now watching her bat her eyes as she tries to wake up. Sheila squints and somehow like a routine she rubs her hands over her stomach.

"What happened? What's going on?"

I don't answer, I just fall down on one knee and grab Sheila's hand.

"James tell me what the problem is? Where's my baby? I was only seven months pregnant. Please tell me that—"

Sheila can't finish. She sees my eyes fill with water like they've done so many times before. She doesn't even let me start talking before she's crying.

"Sheila listen to me. You know that we've gone through some hard times and I know I've hurt you but now it's got to change. I'm gonna change. I got to change."

"James I can't listen to this. Please don't say it. I wanted this child so bad. You don't understand. I love children and I've always wanted a child. I've always wanted to have someone to love and to love me back. You just don't understand, so just don't say it."

"Just listen."

"No. You make promise after promise and I don't want to hear them no mo'. I can't listen to you make me feel like things will be a certain way when really they won't. I can't hear it. You hit me. The first time ever that you put your hands on me."

Sheila turns her body away from me and cries in her pillow. I don't move. I just look up at the ceiling and ask God to give me the strength to get through the next set of events that life is going to throw my way.

"Listen Sheila, I know that you don't want to hear what I've got to say but this is a much needed conversation I'm bout to have wit you. Okay where do I begin? First off, I done you wrong plenty times in the past but you got to know that I always loved you. Nothing or nobody can ever change that. And baby I'm so sorry. I never meant to hit you. Never. You've got to know that I'll never do it again. You know sometimes I don't really know what or why I do certain things. I just don't know. It's like everything's that's happened gets to me. It makes me lose it. It's no excuse for me doing those things to you. You've got to forgive me."

She doesn't move a muscle. She stays with her back to me. I hear her sniffle.

"Listen, I'm saying all this cause I realize that even though I'm grown and old enough to know better, I haven't been acting like a man. Now I promise that I'm going to act, no better yet, be a better man."

"I don't want to hear it."

"Please baby, there's something else. Listen real careful." I pause. "We got to find out if we really gone name our baby boy James Jr. or if you too mad at me."

Sheila turns over and stares at me. Then she starts crying more than before.

"James don't you be playing wit me. Please tell me that you're serious."

"Na baby you know I wouldn't lie to you bout nothing like that."

Sheila keeps on crying but now she's reaching out for me. I kinda crawl to her and we hold on to each other. Lord that feels good. It feels so good to know that we got our son. We finally got what we been praying for. Of course he little but he's here. I cry with her. But this time they're tears of joy. We hold on to each other for a few minutes before we finally let go and wipe the tears from each other's face.

"Sheila I love you so much. Let's do right by this baby."

"We will. I know we will."

Sheila gently kisses me on the lips.

"So where's my baby? I wanna see my James Jr," she says with excitement in her voice.

I stand up, brush the dust off my pants and rush towards the door.

"James wait."

"What's wrong baby?"

"I love you, too."

As I push the door open, my face lights up. I feel a smile appear where there's been a frown for years. And it's about time.

Part 2

Shelia

Aug. 20

Time flies so fast. JJ done started sleeping less and smiling when you talk to him. He's so precious. He ain't got that much color though. I reckon he gone be brown. He light now. I don't care. I'm just so happy that he here. For a while I thought I wasn't gone be able to have children. Wit me losing em everytime, I figured my womb whatn't strong enough. And to think I came close to losing another. When James came in that hospital room, I just knew he was bringing me some bad news. I couldn't even think good thoughts cause I didn't remember much. All I know is that me and James fought. Well he fought me. It was like he went to a whole nother place in his mind. I was scared. Ain't never been scared of him before. But right then, I was afraid. All I member is him choking me and me passing out. Next thing I know, I'm in a hospital bed, not pregnant no more. My mind went a mile a minute. And when I saw James and looked in his face, I could tell that he had been crying.

Right after that I started asking the Lord to help me through. To just make me strong enough to handle the road ahead. I asked for the courage to hear James. Almost the whole time James was talking, I was praying. And when he finally told me JJ was alive, I kept saying in my mind, thank you Jesus. I'm still saying it cause I don't know what I woulda done. Just don't know. Lord knows JJ getting so big. And poor thing his head so funny shaped. It just make me laugh cause it's so cute and I been just rubbing and molding it since we been back home. I was trying to breast feed him but for some reason he don't take well to my milk. I wish he did cause it make me feel close to him when I'm feeding him like that. That's alright though. We doing real good. James ain't been out since we been back cept to go to the store and to the shop every now and then. And you should see how he holds JJ, like that's his pride and joy. He'll just look in his eyes and tickle his face or something and then JJ go to laughing. Well smiling like he looking in the face of some kind of angel or something. I just love seeing them together. It makes me so happy no matter how much my mind wonder off to other places.

Sometimes I think my life is a big test. Some kind of test to see whether or not I'm strong. Strong like my momma. I know I ain't but I sho believe that God just testing me. And He been doing it since I was born. Like He ain't gave me a bit of slack till now. Right now is probably the only little bit of peace I done had since I can remember. But I know it'll only last for a minute. Not longer than that cause I been so worried about JJ. Sometimes I just be so scared. Like when James be holding JJ, I tell him everything to do like hold his head up and hold his back. James gets mad at me when I do stuff like that. But I can't help it. In my mind this is too good to be true. In my mind something gone come and take my joy and it probably gone be my fault.

Ruthie

"RUTHIE BABY, DINNER will probably be ready in a minute."

"Okay," I holler back. I don't say anything else. No exchanges, no objections. I finally realize that I need him. And it's funny because we haven't said two words about being or not being together. All I know is that he's been here and has been supportive of me since the surgery, which was months ago. And I don't mean just being with me but waking up with me when I get up crying in the middle of the night, cooking dinner almost every evening, fixing me a bath. He's doing everything I ever imagined and much more. It's like this procedure scared both of us. It scared the shit out of me but it seems like for him there was something else he felt. Something else that made him come to my rescue.

"Ah Ruthie."

"Huh."

"Ruthie."

"What's up baby?" I say as Chris slowly walks in the room.

"I accidentally burned the pot roast or something."

I try not to laugh but we both look at each other and a smirk falls upon both our faces.

"It's alright, I'll still eat it."

"No you won't. Not this one. I don't know what happened. It's real dark like I burned it but that ain't the worse part. It's as hard as a damn rock."

"Well baby the other night, you did real good with the spaghetti. Now that was real good."

Again we both laugh while the phone rings.

"Hello."

"Yeah, may I ask who's calling? How are you? Good. Okay, hold on. Ruthie telephone."

"Who is it?"

"It's Carmen."

"Oh. Hello."

"So you got him answering the phone now."

"What?"

"You heard me."

"Ruthie, don't mean to interrupt but I'm gonna go grab us something to eat. What cha want?"

"Chicken is fine."

"What?"

"I'm not talking to you so hold on."

"Okay. Mashed potatoes and slaw?"

"Yeah."

"Okay, I'll be back. Is everything okay?"

"Everything's fine."

Chris walks out the door and I look at the phone, take a deep sigh, put the earpiece to my ear while the other end settles on my mouth.

"So you're finally back."

"What do you want?"

"I need to talk to you in person and in private."

"Why?"

"I still love you."

"Don't. I have a man who loves me and that's how it's supposed to be."

"Why because the world or society says so. What about the connection we shared with each other. The love we had for each other."

"Listen don't give me that world bullshit. I didn't make the rules I just try to do my best to play the game. Besides when I was willing to be with you, against the world, you broke the rules. You showed me how this game is really played."

"Well, I'm not calling to fuss but I'm staying at the Marriott for a little while to sort things out. Here's my number. Maybe we can at least have dinner."

"Whatever. What's the number?"

Not knowing why, I write down the seven-digits. They're just numbers on a piece of paper.

"Well hopefully I'll hear from you soon."

"I don't know."

"Just think about it."

"Yeah."

"Talk to you soon."

"Bye."

My mind wanders for a while as I put the phone on the receiver. No matter how hard I try I still have unresolved feelings for her. As much as I try to deny it, I need to know what could have been. Back when me and Henry were together, I didn't know what love was until I met Carmen. I loved him but it wasn't the same. My connection was with Carmen. We started spending a lot of time with each other but at times I didn't feel right. Neither did she. It was new and different. I remember the first time we made love. It was amazing. Nothing I'd ever experienced with Henry. With him it was pumping really hard and fast and then falling to sleep. No pleasure at all. But Carmen kissed me first. Made me feel things I had never felt before. She was gentle and passionate. Her hands touched me like they knew exactly what to do and where to go. She caressed my body and her fingers were gentle. I thought I was having a breakdown the first time she put her tongue between my legs. I felt my body convulse and shake the moment I felt her breath. She held my hands and afterwards me. That's where it started. An innocent night of studying, talking, and crying, turned in to one of the best sexual experiences of my life. After that night we continued being lovers. No one ever found out. Well Henry accused me but I denied it. I'm sure deep down he knew. After Henry and I broke up, Carmen and I continued seeing each other. Even after her sudden marriage to her then boyfriend, we were still together. It wasn't until she had her child and I got in an accident that I finally woke up.

"Ruthie, I'm home, and I got some good ol fried chicken."

Chris's voice breaks my concentration and brings me back to reality.

"Oh really," I say trying not to sound preoccupied.

"Kentucky Fried Chicken was packed. Everybody must have burned dinner. And I swear they were all men."

"Yeah, right."

"I'm serious baby."

We both share a flirtatious grin before digging into the red and white box with our bear hands.

After dinner and after we both have been in bed for about an hour I lean over and rub my fingers across Chris's arm. I gently kiss his back and then caress the back of his neck. He turns around and starts kissing me too. He starts by touching my lips with his, then he moves to my neck and then to my chest and then to my stomach. He goes downtown and stays long enough for me to believe that God is real and for me to call His name a few times. When he comes back up, he kisses me more but stops.

"What's wrong?"

"Are you sure, you're ready?"

I don't say anything. I grab his face and pull it closer to me. I turn him over, climb on top of him and ease my body down on his to return the favor. After I'm done I allow him to enter inside me while I'm on top. We kiss more. I move slow and steady. His eyes are closed and he looks like he's in heaven. Soon he opens his eyes and looks me in the face. His expression is intense as his eyes stare into mine. Then he sits up and kisses my lips. He kisses me more passionately than ever before. He grabs my hands and entwines each finger between the other. We both hold on to each other while both our body's sync together. He grabs me tighter.

"Ruthie, I'm about to—"

With a forceful release, he wraps his arms around my waist and buries his head my chest. When we are both finished, he lies behind me and holds me. Tight, like he never wants to let go.

*****

The bright glare in the window is the only thing I see as the yellow taxi pulls up at the corner of Market and 24th street. I'm nervous, scared, and mad all at the same time. Nervous because I'm going to see a woman I was once in love with, scared because I feel like I'm cheating on Chris and mad because I've allowed myself to get off early from work just to meet her.

I open the door and hand the driver a ten-dollar bill. He quickly hands me my change. *No tip*, I think as I grab the ones and step onto the sidewalk. I don't move for a while because I'm stuck. My feet won't move. Suddenly I hear my name.

"Ruthie, Ruthie."

I look over and there she is, facing me. Her hair is in a short cut and she has on jeans and is holding a lightweight jacket. Her shoes are casual and she looks happy. "Come on" she waves with her hands. I slowly shake my feet out of the clump of imaginary mud they are stuck in and walk towards her. She grabs me by the shoulders like that of an old friend and guides me into lobby of the hotel.

"Ruthie thanks for calling me. I'm so glad you could make it. You had me worried for a minute."

Why did I call, I think to myself as we walk pass two white men and a black man who were standing in a circle talking to one another.

"Where are we going?"

"To the hotel restaurant. They have some great food. I've even tried your favorite, Shrimp and Alfredo pasta. It's great, you'll love it."

As we walk inside, I don't talk, I just listen to Carmen ramble on about her job, her son and this sudden need to get away from her family. While we're walking Carmen points to the table she's chosen for us. I sit on the side so my back faces the window. Carmen sits in front of me and hands me the menu.

"Order anything you want."

I stare at the plastic menu. Not reading just staring at the words as they run together before my eyes. I continue looking at the menu so I don't have to look at Carmen. Finally she pulls the thin booklet down and asks me if anything's wrong.

"I'm fine. Where's that dish you were talking about?"

"I knew you'd want that one."

Carmen excitedly points out the Alfredo dish while the waiter walks over to our table.

"May I take your drink order?"

"Yeah. I'll have, well change that, we both will have sweet teas with lemon and the Shrimp Alfredo pasta."

"Soup or Salad?"

Carmen looks at me before continuing.

"Give her a salad without onions, extra tomatoes and cheese with Thousand Island and Ranch Dressing on the side. And I'll have the clam chowder."

"Coming right up," the waiter says after repeating our orders and walking back to the kitchen.

"I see you still have a good memory."

"Yes I do and so do you. That's why you can't look me in the face."

"I can look at you."

"But you haven't."

I slowly lift my head and allow my eyes to meet hers. She's still beautiful.

"See, I can."

"Well if you can still remember what we had and you can look me in the eyes then I know you can't let this moment go. Baby I left Bill. I'm going back to get William next week. I just needed time to get straight. I've been looking for an apartment all week and I think I've foun—"

"Stop, just stop. What does all this have to do with me?"

"Everything. Ruthie for the past three years you haven't been in my life and I've been miserable. I need you and I'm finally ready to be what you needed me to be back then."

"Well it's too late."

"No it's not. You're not in love with that man."

"Just hush."

"Why, cause I'm telling the truth?"

"Shhh."

The waiter walks over and sits my salad in front of me and Carmen's soup in front of her. He then goes over and grabs our drinks and puts them down. He also places a basket of rolls in the center of the table and glances from my face to Carmen's.

"Is everything okay ladies?"

"Just fine," I blurt.

The waiter walks off and I start wiping off my silverware. I quickly pour both salad dressings on my salad before mixing them together. Carmen does nothing. She simply looks at me and laughs.

"What?"

"I see you still do things the same. When you're upset or nervous you start trying to avoid the subject."

"I'm not nervous or upset. I just don't understand you. You want things when you want and how you want them. On your terms, when you're ready," I say as I stuff lettuce in my mouth. "You don't understand that you aren't the only person who has to make decisions. One person does not make a couple."

"You're absolutely right. I was wrong. I wanted my cake and eat it too. Besides that, I wasn't ready for what you wanted but now I am. Now I know what it takes. We can be happy."

There's a brief moment of silence before I feel eyes digging into me. I look up at her from the depths of my plate and we both start laughing. I finally stop long enough to feel what I imagine to be light peach stuff smeared around my mouth.

"Don't even say anything," I say as I grab my napkin and wipe my mouth. When I put the napkin back on the table, Carmen grabs my hand and squeezes it tightly. Not too tight but tight enough for me know she's there.

"Alright ladies here are your entrée's. The plates are a little hot so be careful."

Carmen lets go of my hand. I look down at my plate and smile because I know this is going to be one of the best Shrimp Alfredo dishes I've had in a while. We immediately start eating and after a while, we slowly begin to talk. After finishing our dinner, we move on to talking more but also reminiscing. By the time we finish our dessert we're laughing. It feels like we're old friends again.

James

LORD IT FEELS so good to have my son in my house and in my bed most of the time. Hell he spend just as much time laying in the bed with me as Sheila. Sometimes me and Sheila get the chance to do the nasty in his room. Now ain't that some shit. JJ done made it so that his daddy got to go out his own bed just to get some loving. It's okay though cause I love him. Sometimes I can just hold him and look at him and talk to him half the day. Especially when Sheila ain't around. Most of the time she's home and she's real particular about holding him. Sometimes she gets to the point where she'll take him from me if I have him too long or if he's crying. And she always got to be the one who feeds him. That shit really gets on my nerves. I don't say too much but sometimes I just want to scream at her and tell her "let me do it." But instead of saying anything, I leave. Like today. I was gonna stay home from the shop and help clean up and stuff but she kept getting JJ from me every time he was a little fussy. And I told her that the boy gone cry a little bit but to just leave him alone. Sheila almost bit my head off and spit it out while I watched her. Then she told me I didn't know what I was talking bout. I got two younger brothers and a younger sister so I ought to know a little bout taking care of a child specially if I had to help raise them. I just walked out the door and decided to come here. I guess it's my spot now. I thought I could stop coming after JJ was born but it's no use.

It's just that there's always something going on. Always something bothering me and on my mind. Besides Sheila getting crazier and crazier every day, I still have nightmares about Vietnam, and on top of all that, Mae done had her baby. All this shit I done created for myself makes me feel like coming out here is gonna help. But the Mae thing I can handle. Kinda. I did sneak by to see her one-day. Just to see if it was true and sho nuff the little boy look just like me when I was a baby. He dark skinned, chubby, big hands and feet, slanted eyes. He mine alright. Look more like me than JJ do. That's what scares me. JJ mine and I know it but he ain't got my color or nutin. He look like Sheila but I do want him to darken up a little, like Mae's boy. Hell I don't even know the boy's name. She never said and I never asked. All I did was look at him and told her he was handsome but that I couldn't have no parts of him. She looked like she was gone cry. Her face kinda stiffened and she closed her eyes. And as much as it gone hurt me to know I got another child out there that I ain't got no parts of, it has to be like that. I did hand her bout $50 so she could get him something. Maybe some pampers and an outfit. I'll probably still leave her something in the mailbox every now and then but Sheila can't know cause I'm scared it's gonna kill her. She know something ain't right but she won't say nothing. Hell I don't blame her cause I don't talk bout nothing neither. We both try to deal wit everything on our own. She writes in that journal and I come here to *Lucky's* and get high.

At least once a week I find myself driving the long way down here. I don't know if I drive the long way to avoid running into people on the way or to convince myself not to go through wit it. It don't matter cause not once have I turned around or passed *Lucky's*. No, instead of working or going to pick up groceries from the store, I end up right out here riding down this dirt road looking for some way to avoid everything. Most of the time it works but last month I was short on my light bill and I had to borrow money from Charlie. Sheila don't know. She don't know a lot that's why I'm here and not home.

I'm backing into the parking lot for the second time this week. The second time. That surprises me in a way cause this is definitely a step up from last week and the week before but it's okay cause at some point I'll stop. I'll definitely stop coming to this hole but for now it's just something to ease my mind.

"Hey James, what's up man?"

"Nothing much, just out here to see Slim."

"He round back."

"Thanks man."

I walk around the building feeling a little ashamed because I just admitted to Fred that I'm here to see Slim. And everybody know what Slim do. He drives the nicest car, wears the shiniest gold chains and fanciest suits anybody's ever seen. Most of the church folk hate him cause of what they think he doing to the community. I used to feel sort of the same way till I had some of what he was selling. Now I see why people like it so much. But I won't ever be one of those men walking round begging people for a dollar just to get a hit. I got my own money and I support any habit I got. Hell I still smoke cigarettes even though they done went up and I damn sure still drink. Hell I got a pint of Brandy in the house. So when I can't afford it, I'll stop. Simple as that.

"What's up?"

"Shit. How's it going?"

"Good, real good but I'm shocked to see you back twice in one week," he says in between taking puffs on a newly rolled joint. He holds the joint toward me as if to offer me some. I shake my head. "So what's up man?"

"Well, I just need something to take the edge off. I'm just a little stressed out and can use a little something today."

"Well listen here, I got something else that might do the trick."

"Slim, I ain't got no extra mon—"

"Before you even say it, I got you. This one is on me. Keep your money, I just want you to feel good, my brother."

"Okay so what is it?"

"Heroine."

He opens his trench coat and pulls out a needle. He holds it in the air like it's a new shinny rock that he found.

"Man I ain't bout to start that shit. Sticking shit in my arm."

"Come on. How you gone pass up free drugs? Shit I know you ain't gone do that so just hush and give it a try. Listen, this here gone do the trick. Trust me, I wouldn't steer you wrong. You my nigga. You always pay me and you don't be asking for no hook up and you a regular so just take my advice, use this whenever you want and if you don't like it then don't worry. Just don't buy it but if you do, come back and see me, I'll be here."

Slim tries to give me the liquid filled needle. I slowly take it but don't say nothing. I give him a nod and walk back to my car. As I get in and sit down I notice my hand is shaking. Almost as if I'm getting anxious because I haven't had any drugs today. I grab both hands with the other and squeeze hard. After rubbing them together for a while, I put the key in the ignition and crank the caddy. At first she's a little hard to start but I keep patting the gas until the engine roars. I drive out the dirt parking lot and go to the shop. This time I take the short route.

When I walk in the shop I rush to close the door, lock it and then I go straight to the bathroom. I don't turn on any other lights besides the ones in the bathroom. I sit on the toilet and pull the needle out my pocket. I begin rolling up the sleeve of my left arm. I grip the needle with my teeth while beating on the vein of my arm with my index and middle fingers. No vein.

"Come on," I say aloud as I look around the bathroom for something to tie around my arm. Nothing. I keep beating. The vein that comes is small but big enough. I gently let the needle fall out of my mouth into my fingers. I position it in my right hand so that it's ready to go in my vein. I keep my fist balled up. When I look down it isn't there anymore.

"Fuck."

I put the needle on the corner of the sink and start beating more. It's no use. I quickly leave the bathroom and go into the shop. I feel on the counter but there's nothing. Then I start pulling stuff out the drawers. Nothing. My heart is racing. Then I remember the rope in my trunk. I run outside. No keys. I go back inside but can't remember where they are. I walk to the bathroom then back into the shop.

"Damn, damn, damn."

I keep looking. Finally I pat my leg and feel them. There they go, I say as I feel a big smile creep across my face. I pull them out my pocket, go back out to the car, and stick the key in the trunk lock. It opens. I fumble through a whole lot of junk. A tool kit, some of Sheila's old clothes that she wants me to give away, papers, and other bullshit till I finally see the piece of rope I was gone use as a clothes line to replace the other dusty rope that's out in the yard now. I grab the rope and run to the bathroom. Finally, I can do this right. I sit down on the toilet and tightly tie the rope around my arm. It's kinda long but now isn't the time to be trying to cut it in half or nothing. So I do the best I can. It works cause the vein is showing again. Green and thick just like it's posed to be. I hold my hand in a fist and grab the needle off the sink. I close my eyes and ease the needle in the center of the vein. At first it stings but after it goes all the way in and I sit for a while I feel it. The needle stays in my arm as my other hand falls to my side. It feels like I'm up in the clouds somewhere. Just floating. My eyes close again. I swing my arms a little bit like I'm swatting a fly. After a few minutes everything calms down. This time because I think I'm high. High in the air. My body shakes a couple of times before I just become numb and still. I feel like I'm in heaven.

Shelia

Lord everything done been perfect. I ain't never been so happy in my life. James been cutting hair out the house sometimes so he can be home wit us. Well it's been kinda perfect. For some reason I just can't help but feel bad bout something. Even though everything good it's still all messed up. And this time its all my fault. I'm the one that did this to our lives. I done made a mess of everything. At first I tried to ignore it but now, I can't. I mean James don't really do that much but when he comes home he acts different. And it's like that all the time. At least 3 times a week. And I know it got something to do with me. He don't know exactly what I done but I do and it's eating me up inside. He gone be hurt no matter what. I just don't know what to do. I love him so much that it's crazy. Sometimes I feel like he the only thang keeping me sane in this here world. But what I did is unforgiveable, even though he done his share or stuff to me. He done cheated, done hit me, he did everything wrong to me but he still did everything right. At least in my opinion. He married me, he's stuck by me, way more than he's not, even when he had good reason to leave. But this time I know he gone leave me. I wouldn't blame him cause I deserve it.

Oh yeah Mae had her baby, too. She had her's bout a month or so after me. She telling people round town that it's James baby. The funny thing is, if she right and that is his baby, then that the only baby he got.

John

"EDNA YOU ready."

"Almost. I just got to put on my lipstick."

"Well, hurry we gone be late."

I stand in the living room waiting on Edna to come out. It didn't take me no time to put on a pair of pants and shirt. Hell we only going over Sheila's to have dinner. It ain't even no big deal but Edna. She got to put on makeup, comb her hair, struggle to put on stockings without tearing em'. And all for what. So we can go sit over Sheila's house and play wit the baby. He ain't gone do nothing but get slobber all over the place and throw up on us. That's why I ain't getting all dressed up but women, they got to put on all this and that. Maybe it's because this is really the first time I'm introducing her to my daughter. She's so proud. When I told her Sheila invited both of us to dinner her face just sort of lit up.

"You ready yet?"

"Here I come."

When Edna walks out she's smiling again. She looks real pretty. She got that red lipstick on with her cheeks all rosy. I ain't never seen her look like that before. She even got curls in her hair, all over.

"Well I'm out here now so lets go."

"You know you really do look nice Edna."

"Thanks John."

With that, we go get in the truck and ride over to Sheila's house. Once we get there I park on the grass and hurry to open Edna's door. We walk up to the house hand and hand. Damn it's been a long time since I held a woman's hand. Annabelle would take her hand away from me when I tried to hold it like she was ashamed to hold my hand. But Edna likes it. She reaches for mine sometimes. Even when we just sitting down watching TV.

I ring the doorbell. Nobody comes. I ring it again. We wait. After bout five minutes of standing here looking around Sheila comes to the door. She looks like she's been crying. I let go of Edna's hand.

"What's wrong baby?"

"Oh, nothing daddy, nothing at all."

"You look. You look like you been crying."

"Oh no daddy, I'm fine."

Sheila looks at Edna. She smiles.

"I'm sorry for being rude. I'm Sheila. You must be Edna."

"Yes. It's nice to finally meet you."

"Nice to meet you too. Why don't y'all come on in?"

We go inside the dark house.

"So where my grandbaby at?"

"Oh, I just put him to sleep that's what took me so long. Dinner almost ready though. I fried some chicken, cooked some rice, collards, and made some biscuits. Nothing big, just a lil something so y'all won't be hungry. I don't know where James at. He said he was coming right back. But you know how that is. He say one..."

Whenever my baby start babbling like that, she scared or something bothering her. When she was little and she was bout to get caught in a lie or something she'd just keep talking. Wouldn't shut up till I hollered real loud or took off my belt. I wonder why she going on like this now.

Edna and I sit down on the couch and listen to her talk. She goes on and on about JJ and how big he getting and how much he growing and how happy she is. After a while she quiets down and announces that the food is done. Me and Edna stand up and go to the kitchen table. By the time we sit down, I hear James coming in the house. He looks sort of strange when he sees us.

"Hey there James. How you?"

"Oh, ah, I didn't know y'all was gone be here. I'm alright though."

"Well James this is Edna."

He staggers over with his hand extended.

"Nice to meet you. I'm James, the man of the house."

"Nice to meet you too."

"You did good John," James says to me after tapping me with his elbow. I stare at him. Something ain't right in his eyes. They look kinda glassy. It takes everything in me not to get up and knock him in the face but I stay cool and turn my attention to Sheila.

She's almost in tears now. Her whole facial expression done went to having this sour look on her face. I try to break the uneasiness that done built since James walked in.

"Thanks James man. I think I done good for myself too."

James don't even blink, he just turns around and leaves the room. Sheila stands in the kitchen a while longer looking like her world's crumbling before her. Edna looking a little off too. Her face done went from being happy to sad. I shouldn't have never brought her over here.

"Daddy, Edna, sorry bought that but James been having a hard time. Money been tight and the baby and me—"

"Don't you say anything, I understand. I'll just fix me and Edna something to go and you and James can have the house to yourselves. Okay."

"I'm so sorry daddy."

"Don't be. Ain't that right Edna? It just gives us more time to spend together."

"That's right baby. We can spend another day together. I don't mind. I'll fix me and your daddy's plates now."

Edna stands up and goes to give Sheila a hug. Sheila's crying by now and after she embraces Edna she runs to the back of the house.

"I hate that man. He's always putting Sheila through this bullshit. Always making her feel bad. I knew this baby wasn't gone make him be a man. He ain't no more of a man than I'm a boy."

"Calm down John, let them work it out. Sheila'll be fine. Now I'll just fix our plates and we can go on back home."

As Edna picks up two of the plates that are already sitting on the table, we hear loud talking coming from the back room.

"Here they are back there fussing and I'm up here trying to fix a damn plate of food. I'm going back there. Ain't no way I'm gonna go home knowing that this man not in his right mind and gone leave him here with my daughter. You must think I'm crazy."

I stand up and walk towards their bedroom.

"No John, wait."

"Wait for what. On him to hurt my little girl again. Hell no, he'll have to kill me first."

As I get closer to room, I hear Sheila pleading with James. She's asking him what's wrong and why he's acting the way he is. I'm only a few feet away from their bedroom. I slowly peek my head around the half shut door and walk in.

"Sheila everything alright back here."

"Yeah daddy, we'll be out in a few minutes."

"James, how about me and you have a talk real quick."

"No daddy that ain't necessary. We alright. Everything just fine."

"Baby, it's alright, I just want to talk to James. Alone."

I walk further in the room until I'm standing right in front of James.

"Listen John, everything fine."

"Yeah I know but hey let's just go outside and chat for a few minutes."

"I said everything was fine," he says as he tries to turn away from me.

Out of nowhere I hit him. It musta just been a reaction cause next thing I know we both fighting. He done bulldozed me into the wall and now we struggling on the floor. Once I push him enough and get on top, I punch him in the jaw. This son-if-a-bitch done made me so mad that I just keep hitting him. I can hear Sheila and Edna somewhere far in the background screaming and asking me to stop. I can't. I keep hitting him. James just laying wit his arms up in the air trying to block the blows. For a while I think I may just be able to kill him but just as my fist is about to hit him again, I stop. It's not because of the hand that's touching my shoulder, or the soft whisper of Annabelle telling me not to do it anymore, but it's the pain that's piercing in my chest. It's the pain that makes my arm stop in mid-air and my body fall over beside the foot of the bed.

Ruthie

"RUTHIE I NEED to talk to you."

"Okay"

"I don't know how to say this."

"Just go ahead baby."

"I went by your job the other day but the secretary told me you took a half day."

"Oh, I'm sorry I didn't tell you but I had a doctor's appointment."

"And what about the other week when you took a personal day."

"What are you spying on me now?

"Do I need to?

"Listen I don't have to tell you everything I do."

"I'm not asking you too but I am asking that you at least be honest with me."

"Honest about what."

"You don't want to marry me."

"What, Chris? What the hell are you talking about? What gave you that idea?"

"Don't try that. I know you've been seeing someone else. I can tell. We don't make love anymore, we don't do anything cause you're always out. Either with Carmen or you're sneaking around not going to work."

"What? Hell we just had sex the other night but because you ain't getting as much as you want I'm cheating."

"No and you know that's not what I meant. But you've been lying to me and now you're gonna make this be my fault. Sex isn't the reason I'm with you but I also know when something's not right. And you aren't the same."

"I am the same but you know what I don't have to stand here and listen to you tell me that I'm sleeping with someone else when I know I'm not."

"Where are you going?"

"Out. I don't feel like fussing tonight."

"Ruthie, wait, let's just sit here and talk about this rationally."

"I'm done talking," I say as I grab my coat and purse, and walk out the door. Chris follows me for a while until I pick up the pace, stop a cab, and jump in. "He's so off base" I say as the cab driver asks me "whereto."

"Just drive."

With no destination we drive for about fifteen minutes until I see the hotel that Carmen's in.

"Stop here."

I jump out the cab and gradually walk up to the hotel entrance. I push the revolving door and step into the opening. As it turns, I walk out the door and travel to the elevator. I push the up arrow. It opens. I step on and then press 10. I've never been up to her room but I know the room number. I wonder if Chris is right. Maybe I don't want to marry him. Maybe Carmen and I are back to where we need to be and I've been playing with Chris just to pass time. I get off the elevator and walk down the hall. Room

1013. I stand in front of the door without moving. Finally, I knock. I hear footsteps.

"Who is it?"

"Me."

Carmen greets me with a smile.

"What's wrong? What are you doing here?"

"Chris and I just got into an argument."

"About."

"He thinks I'm cheating on him."

"Men. Come on in. I was just about to eat dinner. Have some."

"No thanks, I'm not hungry."

"Well, just have a seat. I'm going to be getting packed up cause tonight is my

last night here. It's been months since I left home and I'm ready to get settled again."

"So you're finally moving into that apartment."

"Yeah. I told you that it was over between Bill and I. As a matter of fact I met

with my divorce lawyer today and I'm really gonna do it."

"Are you sure?"

"Sure about what, the divorce. Sweetie that was over before it even started. I

know who I am and now it's time to move on and you should do the same. Figure out

what you want. I believe that you love me and want to be with me but that takes

sacrifice. I'm willing but are you?"

"I don't know. I do love you and I understand what you're saying but I still care

a great deal for Chris. He has seen me through a lot and he loves me."

"Yeah but are you in love with him?"

"I don't want to talk about it anymore, I just want to lay down and rest my eyes."

"Fine. You go get in bed and I'll talk to you in a little while."

Carmen creeps into bed, while I'm pretending to be asleep. Once she's completely underneath the blanket that I'm covered with she turns her body towards me. I don't move. I feel her hand slightly caress my neck. Then I feel her slide closer to my back until she's gently touching me. She uses her fingers to stroke the nape of my neck while she softly presses her lips on me. A chill goes through my body. I'm very still until her kisses become a little more aggressive and she turns my face to hers and starts to kiss me on the lips.

"No. I can't."

"Baby, I know it's been a while but this is right. It feels right."

"No it doesn't. I can't. This just isn't—"

I get out of the bed, stuff my feet into my shoes and head for the door.

"Wait Ruthie, please."

"I can't, I don't belong here. I'm sorry."

I run out the door and take the same route I did when I came up to her room. When I get downstairs I see Chris sitting in the lobby with his eyes closed.

"What? Chris."

"Ruthie, wait before you say anything, I'm here because I have something to tell you."

188 Jennifer N. Shannon

"But how did you know I was here?"

"I saw you here a while ago eating with Carmen and I figured this is where you'd be. I just got here a few minutes ago. I didn't know Carmen's last name but I was about to—"

"To what? You've been stalking me, following me. Haven't you?"

"No that's not it at all. I was having lunch with a co-worker. You know I work down the street from here. We were walking to get a cheesesteak from Tony's. Anyway that's not why I'm here. I'm not here to argue. After you left there was a call. A call from your sister."

"So you came down here to tell me my sister called."

"Ruthie I didn't come down here to work things out. I knew you would probably be confiding in Carmen. I know how close y'all have gotten again that's why I figured you would come here. Now, if you want someone else I don't want to stand in your way. I'm here because your sister called and said that your father had a heart attack and she thought you needed to know."

"What?"

"I'm sorry. I wasn't following you. How could you even think a thing like that? I just wanted to tell you what was going on with your family."

"I don't know how to feel about this."

"About what?"

"About my father. I mean the man that I've always known as my father."

"Damn Ruthie don't be so selfish. This is your dad. Or at least the man that you know as your dad so have some compassion."

"I know. Listen can we go."

"You know Ruthie, I love you but I'm not going to be put on the back burner every time you're feeling depressed or upset. It pisses me off that you came here instead of staying home so we could work things out. But forget it, I'll take you home and then I'm going to pack my things. I'm tired of going through the same thing."

"Chris, I'm not cheating on you. Really. Please don't walk out on me now. I need you and yes, I love you too. I don't want anyone else but I've been going through some things but it's not what you think. I haven't been cheating on you. I've been spending more time with Carmen while she's dealing with her divorce with—"

"With who?"

"Ah Carmen when did you walk in?"

"Just now. So you've been helping deal with—"

"Listen that's neither here nor there. Chris came to tell me some news about my dad."

"Hi Chris how are you? What's wrong with your dad?"

"Hi Carmen. Her dad just had a heart attack and I figured she would be here. Oh and I'm sorry to hear about your divorce."

"Listen baby lets go on and get out of here. I'm tired and I really need to go and call Sheila before it gets too late. Carmen I'll talk to you tomorrow. Okay?"

She doesn't respond. I quickly walk towards the revolving door but not without first looking back at Carmen. She's standing watching me with pleading eyes. Mine are pleading too. The moment I laid in her bed I knew I couldn't be with her. I knew then I had either outgrown those feelings or I just had outgrown her. Either way the only person I could think about was Chris and I pray to God she doesn't tell him about what happened between us then or what could have happened now.

Shelia

Lord my daddy done had a heart attack. James look like he done been beat by a bull or something and now Ruthie back home. She even bought her man with her. They just gone be here for a few days but he drove her down here the other day. Everything just a mess. I feel like I'm bout to die. I can't get control. I know everything gone blow up in my face. My husband gone find out about the baby and then I been having these dreams. Two of em. In one JJ just keep looking at me crying and then JJ real daddy come in. He standing there smiling and JJ looking just like him. Then after a while James walk in holding Mae's baby. After that I wake up sweating. I done had that dream at least everytime I close my eyes. It feel like it's a sign that I got to tell James the truth. But then I have another dream. I only had it bout two or three times but in this one I'm young. Me and Ruthie at least ten and nine but she crying. I see her and my daddy. She crying then she laying on the floor. Next thang I know me and my daddy talking and he making me promise not to tell.

I sort of member but I swear I don't want too. I swear I don't want to be right about what I think happened. I'm just so scared. That dream might mean that I need to tell Ruthie the truth too. I'm so confused and scared. I think I might need to lay here and close my eyes for a minute cause Ruthie should be coming to get me soon. My head keep spinning every time I sit up long enough to do anything and James ain't here and JJ keep crying. I'm so tired. I'm sick of not sleeping at night.

"Hush JJ. Mommy coming."

I just can't get up. My head hurting and this damn book don't help. It don't make things clear in my head. It don't calm me like the doctors told me it would I hate feeling like this I can't stand this. I want to feel better.

"JJ please hush. Just shut up. Shut your mouth."

Damnit why won't the noise stop and the dreams stop and the noise and the baby and eveyrtthing My mind just won't stop. Stop. Who keep talking to me. shut up stop. Be quiet! Lord please please help me keep the voices and noise out my head

*****

They done sent me home already. The doctor's told me I had a mild heart attack but after a couple of days I'm already at the house. They said I need to eat better and get more exercise. Lose some of this unneeded fat. Get rid of the stress in my life. Do this, do that and I should recover. Well if I knew protecting my family was gone cause me to have heart attack I woulda left that man alone. My daughter ain't going nowhere anyway, no matter what happen to me and definitely no matter what happen to her so it's like fighting a losing battle. The only good thing come out of this is Ruthie came home. She even bought her male friend. Ain't that something, everybody I care bout sitting here in the house wit me now. I thought that since last time she was home she wouldn't come back cause of what I told her bout not being her daddy and all. I didn't give her nuff credit cause she came at the drop of a dime to see bout me. Edna done met her and they even get along. Her soon-to-be husband alright too. Hell he way better than James. He seem to treat her right. He drove her all the way down here and even took two days off work. I tell you, Sheila need to take a few lessons cause she still running after James and now I see more than ever that she gone loose it completely. She talking out her head. She probably worried bout where James at. He coulda came over, I ain't gone beat his lil ass no more. I ain't thinking bout him. I'm worried bout my baby girl cause I know she scared and confused. JJ was crying a few minutes ago and what did she do cept left him on the couch while she went in the kitchen to talk to Edna and Ruthie. Like she didn't even hear the boy. When I told her to come get him, she grabbed one of his bottles stuck it in his mouth and kinda just laid him down. It's not like her to just sit him down like that on the couch, he only a baby. He at the stage where he moving and trying to see where he can go even though he can't go nowhere by hisself.   And I know what's gone

happen. He gone spit the bottle out and just roll over and off the couch.

"Sheila don't leave him like that."

"Daddy I know what I'm doing he'll be fine, I'm just running out here to get

him a pamper."

As soon as she turns her head good, sho nuff here he go tumbling off the couch.

"Hush JJ, it gone be alright, I'm coming right back."

"Sheila you ain't gone pick him up first, can't you see he crying like he done

hurt hisself."

"Daddy I'm sick of you telling me how—"

"I got him. Come here JJ, it's alright baby," Ruthie says as she runs out the

kitchen into the living room and grabs JJ.

"Sheila I ain't trying to tell you nothing but you ain't gone sit here and let that

baby fall off the couch just cause you worried bout that drug addict husband of yours."

"Come on now y'all. Daddy I got JJ. He fine and real soon everybody can eat."

"No Ruthie you don't have to come here and try to help me out. I'm fine. And

my husband ain't no drug addict, he just having a hard time."

"Girl you so blind you can't see what's right in front of you."

"I can see a whole lot, just like I could back when we was little."

"Child please. You talking crazy."

"I ain't talking crazy and I'm sick of everybody thinking I'm crazy. I'm not.

Besides I know a lot more than you want me to say. Ain't that right daddy?"

"Just hush Sheila cause you talking that crazy talk again."

"No I ain't he just don't want Ruthie to know what really happened that night."

Ruthie walks back in the living room but not without giving JJ to Edna first.

"What really happened when? What are you talking about? What night?"

"Nothing forget I even started it."

"No. I'm sick of being in the dark. Tell me what you're talking about."

"No, just hush Sheila."

"No daddy, you hush, it's been too long and it's time for Ruthie to know what happened to her when she was ten years old after you beat her to the point where she passed out."

Sheila walks over and grabs Ruthie by the hands. They both sit down on the long couch that's across from me. I can't move. I sit and watch Sheila as she starts something I wish I could take back more than anything else.

"Yeah, Ruthie member that night when momma was out of town and we was home wit daddy playing at night when we was posed to be sleep."

"I remember. Daddy called me up to the front of the house cause he always beat me if we did something wrong. Chris this is the dream I keep telling you bout," she says as she looks over at her friend and then back at me.

"That's right. He always beat you and not both of us. Ain't that right daddy?"

"Why don't you just hush, trying to stir up trouble," I say trying to get up but Edna puts her hand on my shoulder as if to tell me to just sit here and take whatever's coming next.

"Well Ruthie, when daddy called you up there, I laid in the bed and wondered why he always whooped yo butt and never mine. I laid there and listened to him fuss and holler at you. And you didn't say much, just said yes and then that was it. But when I heard him hit you that first time I jumped up. He hit you so hard. It was like he was taking everything that he felt out on you in that one hit. So he kept hitting you and I got out the bed. I watched for a while and then I went back in the room. But when I didn't hear you crying no more, I came back out. It was like you just blacked out or something cause by the time I got to the door, I saw daddy and he was..."

By this time, I'm crying and still trying to get up but Edna's holding me down. My mouth's frozen cause I can't say nothing.

"He was what, Sheila?"

"He was....he was touching you in your private part."

"What?"

"Hush, Sheila, just hush wit these lies."

"I ain't lying. I saw you. You was touching Ruthie and then you kissed her neck. You probably was already done cause you was pulling up her panties when I saw you. And you saw me too. Ain't that right daddy?"

"Just hush Sheila, just h—"

"Hush why? Cause I'm telling the truth. You saw me and told me not to say nothing to nobody. You made me keep this secret of yours for all these years and I hate you for it."

"Wait Ruthie, don't go, let me explain," I say as I reach up for her as she passes the recliner. She jerks away and glares at me through tears. Through tears that say I'm more than mad at you. I hate you, you disgust me, I despise you. She keeps walking and I look over at Sheila who looks like she's more confused now than when she started this damn conversation.

"What's going on? Why Ruthie leaving, dinner'll be ready in a little while."

"You really are going crazy. Look at what you done. Ruthie hate me now and I didn't rape her. I couldn't—"

"Couldn't do what daddy? Where Ruthie going? Did I say something wrong? Lord, where JJ? Where JJ daddy?"

I don't even look at her. I can't. She's talking to herself and wondering what she did wrong. I can't believe she told. The thing that hurts isn't so much that she let it all come out but that she looks just like her mother did that night. Like she's fighting and holding on to the same thing, at the same time.

I struggle to get up and walk to my room. Ruthie and her friend left cause I heard the car pull off. I sit on the edge of the bed and look in the mirror. I feel like a fool. A fool who has just lost one daughter that wasn't really his to begin with and another whose mind has driven her away. A fool who practically did the same thing to his child that some dirty white man did to his wife. A fool who has been living with this for 20-something years but who has lived long enough to know that whatever's done in the dark will surely come to light.

James

SHEILA MUST BE crazy to think I'm a be going over to her daddy house when he done tried to kill me one time. Next time one of us might have to actually die and it ain't gone be me.

Hell I don't even feel like going in my own house. I didn't go home last night so I know Sheila mad at me. I just didn't want to come back. She wanted me to go wit her to be wit her family. I ain't crazy and I know they didn't want me there so me and her got into this big argument then she grabbed JJ and left wit Ruthie. That was good for me cause I didn't have to sit and listen to the bullshit all day. Shit, that man gave me a black eye and almost broke my damn jaw. I wish I would go in his house and eat his food and talk wit him and his family like ain't nothing wrong. I do feel bad that he had a heart attack but it wasn't my fault. He the one who came in the room and minded my business. He the one who jumped on me. If I didn't have no respect for him, I woulda hurt him. Whatever. I'm sick of explaining myself to everybody. Explaining why I'm going out to *Lucky's* all the time, why JJ don't look nothing like me, why Sheila going crazy, why this, why that. The best thing I can do is go get me a hit of something just to keep my mind straight for more than five minutes at the time. Maybe today I can go in this house and not hear the fussing. Maybe just once me and Sheila can talk.

As I walk in the house I holler out Sheila's name. I don't hear nothing. No baby noises, no nothing. I keep walking towards the back. There ain't no lights on. Nobody's here. Good. I'm glad I'm here alone. That means Sheila must have JJ and that means she out with somebody else. She must still be wit Ruthie. I don't really like Sheila keeping JJ by herself a lot since last time I came home and she was laying in the bed while JJ was in his crib crying his eyes out. His eyes and face was red and who knows how long he had been crying like that. And when I asked her why she was just letting him cry she didn't have no explanation, no reason why she was just laying there listening to him. She just seem so distant and lost, like she got something on her mind.

I go over to the side of the bed, kneel down, lift up the mattress and pull out Sheila's journal. Last time there wasn't nothing too interesting in it. I never really wanted to know her private thoughts but it seems like her thoughts are going from being good to downright crazy. I just want to know what's wrong wit her. Whether or not I should be more worried bout leaving JJ here wit her by hisself. Hell I ain't too much better but at least I ain't gone just let the boy cry or be wet or be hungry all day and not do nothing. Something else got to be bothering Sheila that's why I got to read this book, see what she telling it instead of me.

I open the book and flip through a few pages. I hear something. "Damn here they come." I quickly push the notebook back in between the two mattresses and lay on the bed before Sheila gets to our bedroom.

"Hey baby."

"Hey James."

"How you?"

"I'm alright. How you, seeing as though you didn't come home last night?"

"Listen, I'm sorry, I just couldn't cause I knew you would be mad at me cause I wasn't going over your dad's house wit you."

"Well, I don't see why you couldn't come over. The heart attack wasn't your fault so what's the big deal. He done forgave you."

"Listen, maybe next time but it seem like it's too soon to be trying to be friends wit yo daddy and he done fought me a few days before that. Besides the rest of yo family was gone be there and I didn't want them looking at me funny."

"Where you been?"

"Nowhere but to the shop. That's where I stayed."

"I bet."

"Listen, I ain't messing wit no other women and you just gone have to believe that."

"Well what about the drugs? What about you walking round like you high all the time?"

"I ain't walking round no kinda way. I'm fine."

"You fine alright. Well why the light bill was late this month. Again. You don't think I know what's going on but I do. Why you don't never have no money no more?"

"Damnit Sheila a baby expensive. What you expect? We got an extra person to feed and I ain't making no more money than I was before the baby came."

"I understand that but the shop was doing good and I'm working again so it still don't add up. Besides I been hearing stuff."

"What stuff?"

"Just that you been hanging out to *Lucky's* asking for that Slim man. And everybody know what Slim out there doing. I just don't want you to get caught up smoking that stuff like some of them other folks out there."

"Like I said before, I'm fine. I am just fine. Now let me hold my son."

*****

A day ago I found out the man I knew as my dad tried to molest me. Ain't that something? My own father beat me until I fell out and then he touched me. Touched me like a man touches a woman not how a father touches a daughter. What could he have been thinking? Why didn't I know? Why didn't Sheila tell me? My mind's going a mile a minute. I been laying here crying in this hotel since we left the house. I can't even eat. I feel like my whole life is a lie. Everything I knew to be true has turned out to be a lie. No wonder I've been so screwed up. No wonder I have such a terrible relationship with men and a more confusing one with women.

"Ruthie we got to talk."

"About what?"

"About this. You've got to get up and face what just happened."

"You want me to face what just happened. So you mean you want me to talk to my dad. You can't expect me to do that. I hate him too much. I hate that I even came home and that he lived through that damn heart attack."

"Listen baby everything's gone be just fine. Trust me."

"Chris please, not now."

"Okay, but you got to deal with this. We can't stay in this hotel forever. You need to go talk to your dad or at least your sister."

"How do you expect me to go see that man? That man who tried to molest me while I was passed out. He tried to molest me and Sheila saw it all."

"Are you sure she wasn't just making it up or blowing it out of—"

"Making it up. For what. She's telling the truth cause this is the dream I've been having. Sheila helped me see the part I couldn't. The part that I blocked out of my memory or better yet didn't know happened. And to think I wanted to give this man another chance to be in my life. He's sick and I hate him."

"Alright baby, I know it's gonna be hard to see him and I know you don't want to speak to him right now but we've at least got to get our stuff. I'll go get our clothes and then we can drive back home. Maybe after we go home and you cool down, you can deal with everything better."

"I guess you're right. Okay you go get our stuff and then we can go."

"Are you going to be alright here by yourself?"

"I'll be fine."

"Well, you've at least got to tell me how to get to your dad's."

"Don't call him that."

"What, your dad? Listen Ruthie I don't understand everything that's happening but maybe it wasn't as bad as you think."

"Chris I wouldn't expect you to understand. This is supposed to be my daddy and he tried to—"

"I'm sorry baby, come here."

Chris pulls me close to him as I allow my body to relax in his arms. He holds me till my mind calms down and I drift to sleep again.

*****

I'm still not really sleeping none and the doctor's told me to just write down whatever I feel. Yeah they told me that but it ain't working. Last I wrote in this here thang JJ cried till James got home. James was so mad at me. I don't member what happened. All I know is that I heard him but couldn't move. I couldn't get up or nothing. I mean I told him to be quiet and shut up. I had just changed him and he had been feed so I didn't know what else to do. Besides I was tired. I hadn't got no sleep or nothing so I musta just went to sleep. I told James I was sorry but he still won't leave me home with JJ by myself. I'm alright but James don't think so. He think I'm going crazy or something, I guess. I'm fine I just had a bad day. A day that took everything out of me. Everything out my body. But today James here wit us. So he the one that's taking care of JJ. They somewhere round. That's good cause I needed a break. My mind just been going so fast and today I feel like I have a grip on what's going on in my life. I do know that I got to clear my mind bout some stuff so I need to write this down and maybe even tell James. Hell I done spilled everything to Ruthie yesterday and she ain't talked to me since. I hope she don't hate me for not telling her sooner. I wanted to but it finally got to the point where I just couldn't hold it no more just like I can't hold this. I'm shocked I ain't wrote bout this before. I guess before I was so happy bout how things had turned out but now my mind ain't letting me rest. It's like everytime I look round or look at JJ he's looking back at me with those small brown eyes that don't look nothing like James. His complexion kinda light too compared to me and James. And now I believe people saying things like that. They whispering cause I can tell. When they see us in the grocery store they'll be looking at the baby and saying he look more like me and they can't see James nowhere in his face. That really ain't all that true. He look like he might be able to be James baby if his head wasn't so big. I don't think you can really tell just by looking at a baby. I think when they little like that you just got to let em get bigger and then they start looking like somebody. They don't just pop out looking one-way or the other. Like them ol people say, if a baby live in the same house wit a person they start looking like the person they staying wit. Anyway, the reason I know this baby ain't James baby is because everytime I done been pregnant I knew it right after it happened. Something in me just made me know. I just felt it. So I know it ain't his cause I felt that way after sleeping with someone else. For a long time I thought about killing the baby myself. I still think about it sometimes cause I go through more grief bout it than it's worth but burying your own child is the hardest thing in the world. Especially if it's by yo own hand. Me, I ain't never had to physically bury one well we did have a small memorial service for my stillborn so I guess I have. That was hard and I didn't even get a chance to hold him only to love him while he was in my stomach. I know I can't take the life of JJ. If I did I might as well take my life too. Sometimes I wish things could be different. I wish it didn't have to be this way but it is. I just hope James don't hate me forever for it. I can't stay here no more. I need to go speak to my daddy but not till after I get this off my chest.

John

I LOOK OUT the window when I hear the car drive up. I can always tell when someone comes in the yard cause I got rocks on the driveway. I knew it was them before I even heard the rocks being spread out on the soil. I knew they was coming cause they left they stuff. I been waiting every since they left. I let the curtain go back to how it was and just sit back in my favorite recliner. I'm home by myself. I told Edna to go home cause I needed to be alone. I needed to be by myself for this moment right here. I just sit and be patient. I figure Ruthie got to get up the nerve to come in the house since she done found out what I been trying to keep hid.

There's a knock on the door.

"Come in," I yell.

I hear heavy feet press hard onto the floor. I turn around and see her friend instead of her.

"Where Ruthie?"

"She didn't want to see you right now so I'm here to get our stuff."

I don't try to stop him. I just lean back and allow him to pass. I stand up and walk into the kitchen. I look under the sink and feel in the back for my whiskey. I grab it and turn the cap until it comes off. I haven't had a drink in a long time so I know this is going to burn. I finally put the bottle to my lips and turn it up. Damn. I take another gulp before turning around and seeing this young man standing in my face.

"Is there something I can do for you son?"

"No sir," he says after putting the two black suitcases down.

"Well maybe you can. How about telling me what was going through your mind when you felt the need to molest your own child."

I don't say nothing. I just stand looking down at the floor. He picks the suitcases back up and begins to walk past me.

"Long time ago my wife was raped by a white man. She had a baby and that baby was Ruthie. I never once figured out how to deal wit the situation. I never once looked at Ruthie without feeling ashamed of myself and without feeling I was to blame. But my problem was that I couldn't help but be mad at myself and so I took it out on Ruthie. No it wasn't right but that was how I dealt with everything. That was what I did to get through my days. Everyday. The only thing I regret more than my wife getting raped was me turning around and doing the same thing to my child. I don't know what came over me. I just saw her laying there passed out and I started crying. Crying cause this child was made out of hate but she was the most beautiful child I had ever seen. Her face was perfect, her body was without a mark, her complexion was soft, her personality, warm. And that's when I touched her face. I brushed my hand across her skin and before I knew it I had my hand down her panties. I cried harder after I got on top of her. I stopped though. I couldn't do it. And not because of Sheila. She didn't see nothing but me pulling her panties back up. After I looked down at Ruthie wit her tears stuck and dried to her face I pulled my pants back up and just sat beside her rubbing her cheeks.

That's when I saw Sheila. I'm not making excuses but I been holding this in for so long and know this, I woulda took it to the grave wit me but since it's out in the open somebody needed to know what really happened."

"Well, Ruthie's outside and that's who needs to hear this?"

"She don't want to listen to me. If she did she woulda came in here instead of sending you."

"Listen, I understand what Ruthie's going through. You can't expect her to just talk to you after finding out all of this. You can't expect her to be forgiving and run to your arms after this. Come on man. I'm not gonna claim to fully identify and I can see your position. But to touch a child. That's sick. I don't blame Ruthie if she never talks to you again."

He picks up the suitcases and walks out the house, while I stand with my whiskey in hand and tears falling from long ago.

                              *****

When Chris walks out the house, Sheila pulls up. She parks right beside us but she doesn't even look at me. Instead she acts like she's on a warpath. She runs past Chris and goes into the house. By the time Chris gets to the car we both hear screaming. I don't move. Chris opens the door.

"Ruthie we need to go see what's going on. Come on."

I sit for a minute longer as I watch him jog back to the house. I slouch further into the seat but after hearing more arguing, I get out. By the time I make it on the inside, Chris has Sheila's hand and she's letting a knife fall to the floor.

"What's going on?"

"Ruthie, get Sheila, she stabbed your dad."

"What?"

I look over and sure enough he's on the floor by the refrigerator holding his arm, while blood flows from his hand. I grab Sheila while Chris helps him up.

"Are you alright," Chris asks.

"I'm fine, it's only a flesh wound."

I take Sheila to the living room and hold her. She's in a state of shock. Like she doesn't know that she's the one who has tried to kill her own father.

"Baby, what happened? Why did you stab him?"

She turns to me and looks at me with the same flat look in her eyes that I saw the day I went to see her in the hospital.

"Ruthie, what are you talking about? I didn't know you was home. When did you get here?"

I pull her close to me and rub her face. While I'm holding Sheila, Chris helps John onto the couch.

"Is he gonna live?"

"Yes, I'll be fine. She's just upset about everything. She blames me for everything getting so messed up so I don't blame her for this. Sheila's sick and has been—"

"Don't you dare call her sick, you're the one who's sick. I can't even stand to look at you."

"Ruthie why you and daddy hollering at each other? What's wrong? Daddy why you holding your arm like that? What happened?"

"No reason. You know how we always fuss at each other don't you?"

"And my arm is alright, I just fell and cut it."

"Daddy you alright? Does it hurt?"

"No, I'm fine."

"Ruthie it's time for y'all to stop all that and be like real father and daughter. It shouldn't matter what has happened between y'all. Y'all are still family. We all are."

I grab her face and pull her closer to me. After a few minutes of silence she seems to drift off into a light sleep.

"Chris come get her and put her in the car. We need to take her home."

He gently takes Sheila in his arms and walks out. I get up and look over at John.

"You happy now. Now that you've lost both of us."

I stare at the sorrow in his face before turning towards the door and walking out.

James

AS SOON AS Sheila walks out the door and gets in the car I'm back at it. She came outside and saw me and JJ hanging out and said she needed to go over her dad's. I threw her the keys to the car, went inside, gave JJ a bottle, put him in the bed and reached between the mattresses to get that journal. Something has been telling me to read this for a while but I've always put my thoughts aside. Today I have to read what she's been writing.

I walk to the kitchen and sit at the table. I flip through about a dozen entries until I get to one that's after JJ was born.

Aug. 5, 1977

Well, me and James doing good. He been here wit me and the baby and he such a good father. He even stopped taking secret shots of liquor before coming to bed. It feels good for him to want to be sober and him taking this step means a lot and shows me a lot. I love him so much. I really don't have much to say today. Everything's going good in my life so I might as well wait till I really got something to talk about.

For some reason I been feeling kinda down. I mean I feel scared to touch the baby and scared for somebody else to touch him too. I scare myself wit some of the thoughts that come in my mind. I'm scared to death of what I might do. Sometimes I wish I could control what my mind tells me to do. It's like when I did that stuff to myself and had to go to the nut house it was because of stress, I thought. I don't know what this is from. Maybe I'm stressed and don't know it. James don't know how I feel. He think everything fine cause I can really put on a good front. I don't let him know that I'm scared and feel like my world gone fall apart in any minute. I just keep that to myself and in this book.

I feel much better today. I mean I want to write in you everyday but I can't. Some things I have to keep in my mind. Keep that stuff for myself. James so sweet. He took the baby to his mother's house and we went out to dinner. He must be doing good at the shop cause he took me out of town. We went to Rockingham. I just loved it. He make me feel so good. Like he knows when I'm not happy and when the world's on my shoulders. I don't know what I would do without him.

I keep reading but nothing seems out of the ordinary until I get to this entry:

Lord everything done been perfect. I ain't never been so happy in my life. James been cutting hair out the house sometimes so he can be home wit us. Well it's been kinda perfect. For some reason I just can't help but feel bad bout something. Even though everything good it's still all messed up. And this time its all my fault. I'm the one that did this to our lives. I done made a mess of everything. At first I tried to ignore it but now, I can't. I mean James don't really do that much but when he comes home he acts different. And it's like that all the time. At least 3 times a week. And I know it got something to do with me. He don't know exactly what I done but I do and it's eating me up inside. He gone be hurt no matter what. I just don't know what to do. I love him so much that it's crazy...

I quickly browse the rest of that paragraph and jump to the next.

Oh yeah Mae had her baby, too. She had her's bout a month or so after me. She telling people round town that it's James baby.

The funny thing is, if she right and that is his baby, then that the only baby he got.

I don't move. Tears come from nowhere. I squeeze the book tight and almost tear it in half but decide I gotta keep reading. There's got to be more. I keep reading even though the writing is blurry from the water that's either falling on the page or from it being deep in my eyelids. I'm at the last entry in the book. It reads:

This is killing me. This secret. I just can't hold on to it no more. It happened a night or two before James came home that time for I went in the hospital. I member it like it was yesterday. I was sitting in the kitchen waiting on James. While I was tapping my fingers on the table I heard a car pull up in the yard. I didn't even have a chance to turn off the lights like I wanted to. I slowly stood up ready to greet James with the nasty look and whatever words I could think of. But then there was a knock at the door. So I was like who could this be because I knew James had his key. James always had his key cause no matter how drunk he was he got in this house when he needed too. "Who is it?" I said. "It's Charlie" was the answer from the other side. I opened the door and then turned away from Charlie. He followed me on in the house without saying nothing. I tried hard to wipe the tears from my face before he came in the living room behind me. "So how you doing Sheila?" "I'm alright Charlie but James ain't here right now." We was sitting across from each other by now but my head was down. "I know I came to check on you. I seen him the other day and he told me he hadn't been home so I wanted to make sure you was alright." And after that I busted into tears. I just couldn't stop crying. For some reason I just kept crying till Charlie came over and hugged me. He just kept rubbing my shoulders and saying it's gone be alright. So after I had cried enough Charlie just kept holding me. He was a gentle man like that. But this time after I finished crying me and Charlie let go of each other but our faces were looking at each other in a strange way. We just sat there and allowed our lips to come together. He only kissed me once. Maybe it was me. Maybe I started it cause I remember Charlie just sitting there real still like till maybe a few minutes later and then he got into it. We stayed there for a while before stopping. I pulled away this time but only to stand up and grab his hand and take him to the bedroom. I knew it was wrong but I needed him that night. I needed to feel like someone cared about me that night. And not the physical part. I just wanted to feel like a woman. One who was appreciated and I wanted a man who looked at me the way I wanted him too. As I led Charlie in the back he looked at me the way I needed him too. With passion. I was tired of feeling like somebody had just slept with somebody else and was doing me a favor to be sleeping wit me. That's how James looked at me. Like he was only being with me cause he was my husband and it was his duty not because he found me attractive and was turned on by me. But with Charlie that look wasn't there. And when I laid down he looked at me and smiled. Actually cracked a smile but nothing like he was laughing but more like he was happy and wanted me to smile too. He wanted me to be happy. And he made me happy. For once I didn't think bout nothing. Not about no other woman cause he took that away for just a while. He kissed my body and caressed me. He wasn't fast or in a rush. He was gentle and he took his time and watched me. I didn't close my eyes not once while he was making love to me. And neither did he. Just looked in my eyes and kissed my lips until he couldn't take it no more. After that we went to sleep. We didn't sleep long but we did nap off for a while. Charlie had his arms around me and I was snuggled deep in him. After a few hours passed we both were woke but we didn't say nothing. Finally I told Charlie that it was bout time for him to go. He still didn't say nothing, just got up and put back on his clothes. His eyes told me that he wouldn't ever tell James what happened. I listened but didn't say nothing. I walked him to the door and we hugged again before he walked out the house. I listened as he backed out the driveway. Then I walked back to the bedroom and laid in the bed and held on to the pillow. For a little while I had been in peace. Charlie had made me feel like a woman again but after it was over the only thing I could think of was that another night had passed and James didn't come home again. You know what though, when James did come home a few nights later I knew it was too late. He had been gone too long. I had already slept wit his best friend and knew that I could never go back. And then I had this feeling in my gut. My gut, my womanly instinct told me that I was pregnant. Even when I didn't know it, I knew it. And I knew it wasn't James's. God shol do know how to work things out. Cause I woulda never thought this would happen to me but now that I'm thinking about it, it couldn't have happened no other way. This is like the ultimate punishment for James and kinda like the greatest revenge for me.

I can't breathe. As I stand up, the door opens.

"Hey James. We just bringing Sheila home cause she had a little episode over to the house and since we bout to go on back to Philly we just wanted to make sure she got home safe."

I slowly turn around and look at Ruthie and some yellow looking man while they help Sheila in the house.

"Hey baby. I'm alright. I just fell asleep so we gone have to get daddy to— What's wrong?"

I hold up the book. Sheila comes running towards me. She grabs me and cries at my feet.

"What's wrong? James what's that? Why is she acting like that?"

"Sheila why don't you tell your dear sister and her man why you at my feet crying like a baby."

"James lets just talk bout this. What you doing reading that anyway? That's mine. It's mine."

She jumps up and we struggle for the notebook. The man acts like he's coming over but Ruthie stops him. For that second that I look at Ruthie's boyfriend walking over, Sheila gets the notebook. She sits on the floor and holds the book like it's a baby.

"Sheila how could you? How could you sleep wit my best friend, have his child, and then lie to me? I knew something was wrong but I didn't want to think that you could do something like this."

Sheila stands up and faces me. She looks deep into my eyes.

"I'm sorry. I'm so sorry. I never meant for this to happen but you act like I had another choice. I needed JJ just like I needed that night Charlie gave me. I was hurting and no I never meant to do this but it happened. And as much as I tried to hide it and cover it up I knew this day would come. I hate it came to this but I do love you. We can put this behind us and start over now that everything's out in the open."

"Start over. You done went out here and fucked my best friend. JJ ain't mine. He ain't mine. Don't you see? I hate you. I hate I ever met you. I hate I ever fucked you. I hate I ever fell in love wit you. You're nothing to me."

"James don't say that. You don't mean—"

"I do. Yes I do mean it. Everything I'm saying I mean cause it's true. You're dead to me and so is that boy in there."

Sheila grabs me and I push her away. She won't let go so I walk while she falls onto my leg and I drag her through the house.

"Sheila let me go. I'm leaving. I'm getting my shit and I'm getting the fuck out of here."

"No you can't. I love you and JJ loves you."

"I don't love you or him."

She lets go of my pants and then I feel her jump on my back. By this time I reach the bedroom.

"Get off me."

"No. You can't leave me. Not now. We've got the family we want. Everything's fine."

I swing around and then back up into the wall. Sheila slides off me. I decide to leave my clothes. I look back long enough to see Sheila crying with her head in her hands. As I look at her I know this isn't all her fault but I can't stand to be here. I want to reach out to her or maybe even say that I still love her but I can't. She looks up at me long enough to see that maybe there might be hope for us but I turn around and keep walking down the hall. I hear her get up. I thought it was to jump on my back again but she goes and gets JJ. I hear him crying. By the time I get to the kitchen I hear fumbling in the closet like she's pulling everything out. I see Ruthie and the man standing near the sink. Ruthie has tears in her eyes but looks at me like she's just waiting on the right time to step in.

"Ruthie I'm sorry but I've got to go."

She doesn't say anything. She just looks at me and I pat her shoulder slightly as I open the screen door. It's still hanging on its hinges. Still hanging on by a thread. Before I can let go of the door, I hear a pop. The one sound that lets me know Sheila's finally done the unthinkable. I stop in my tracks. I don't turn around. Ruthie's crying. Her and the man rush to the bedroom. I hear Ruthie scream louder. When they come back out, I hear cries. They're from JJ. As I stand in the doorway, I wonder how I would feel if Sheila had just taken JJ's life instead of her own. It doesn't matter. She's dead at the hands of my gun that I always kept hid in the closet in an old shoebox. Damn, Sheila's gone. I let go of the raggedy door, walk down the hill and down the street. For every step I take, a tear falls. I'm not crying but a tear falls each time my foot bears down on the pavement. I don't look back. I just walk and walk until my tears dry up.